P9-DMJ-595

A Simple Act of Kindness

STORIES *from* HOPE HAVEN

A Simple Act OF *Kindness*

PAM HANSON
&
BARBARA ANDREWS

Guideposts
New York, New York

Stories from Hope Haven is a registered trademark of Guideposts.

The characters, events and medical situations in this book are fictional, and any resemblance to actual persons or occurrences is coincidental.

www.guideposts.com
(800) 932-2145
Guideposts Books & Inspirational Media

Cover design and illustration by Lookout Design, Inc.
Interior design by Lorie Pagnozzi
Typeset by Aptara

Printed and bound in the United States of America
10 9 8 7 6 5 4 3 2 1

In loving memory of Judy Ward,
sister and aunt.

The Best Medicine by Anne Marie Rodgers

Chasing the Wind by Patricia H. Rushford

Hope for Tomorrow by Patti Berg

Strength in Numbers by Charlotte Carter

A Simple Act of Kindness by Pam Hanson & Barbara Andrews

Chapter One

CANDACE CRENSHAW RUBBED HER HANDS TOGETHER vigorously, trying to warm them before beginning her morning shift as an RN in Hope Haven Hospital's Birthing Unit. It seemed exceptionally cold for early March, but Deerford, like the rest of Illinois, frequently suffered long, hard winters.

At least she was thankful that her mother would take Brooke and Howie to school. She hated to think of her children waiting in the frigid wind for a school bus. Her heart constricted when she remembered that their father had always been the one to make the school run in the morning. Perhaps someday her grief at Dean's untimely passing would lessen, but the loneliness she felt without him was still with her every day.

Others in her grief-counseling group had said that once the sharp pain of mourning passed, there was still the aching loneliness of loss. Candace was grateful that she had friends in her support group who understood what she was going through; and their leader, Lila Adams, was everything she could hope for in a counselor: wise, kind, and supportive.

It wasn't quite time to sign in on her floor, so she called home from the staff lounge. Her mother, Janet, would have everything under control, and it was nice to say good morning to Howie and Brooke and wish them a good day.

"Are the kids up?" she asked when her mother answered the phone.

"Brooke's in the shower, and Howie's here in the kitchen with me. I think he'd like to talk to you. He had one of his bad dreams."

"Hi, sweetheart," Candace said when her son came on the line. "Do you want to tell me about your dream?"

"I didn't know what car to get in after school." She could hear Howie sniffle.

"You don't need to worry about that. Grammy's always there to pick you up."

"No, Daddy was picking me up, and I couldn't remember what he looked like."

Candace's eyes teared. She wished she were home to hug Howie, but she had to trust her mother to comfort him this morning.

"It was only a dream, sweetheart. By the time you get to school, you'll be too busy to think about it."

"Maybe." He sounded dubious.

"I have to go to work now, but when I get home, let's play Chutes and Ladders before dinner, okay?"

Candace could practically hear him perk up. "Yeah!" he exclaimed.

"Love you," Candace said, wishing her children didn't have to worry about forgetting their father.

When Candace entered the Birthing Unit several minutes later, her supervisor was on the phone. Riley Hohmann was three years older than Candace and several inches taller, and somehow she managed to do her blonde hair in a stylish french twist every morning and still get to work early. Candace kept her wavy brown hair in a chin-length bob that required little fussing, but some days it was still a struggle to get to the hospital by seven, especially if her children were awake before she left.

Riley hung up the phone, and Candace was about to say good morning when a piercing scream sent both women running toward a labor room.

"We're right here, Sue," Riley said in a soothing voice to the young woman on the bed gasping between contractions. "And your doctor will get here in plenty of time."

"It hurts so much," Sue said. "Can't you make it stop?"

Candace was surprised to see the expectant mother alone in the room. Usually a husband, relative, or friend would be there to offer encouragement.

Before either of the nurses could say anything, the patient wailed loudly, "I want Benny!"

"There's been some congestion at O'Hare Airport," Riley explained in a voice that told Candace she'd explained it before. "When your husband's plane can land, he'll get here as soon as possible."

"I hate airplanes! I need him here!"

Her tirade ended in sobs, and Candace stepped up to the bed and gently stroked her hand.

"I understand just how you feel," she quietly said. "I had two children myself, and it seems as if labor lasts forever. But believe me, it doesn't. Before you know it, you'll have a beautiful baby in your arms. Do you know whether it's a girl or a boy?"

"A boy. Benny wants to name him Randall after his father, but I don't like that name. I brought a book of names so we can find a better one—if he ever gets here."

Candace didn't know whether she meant the baby or the father, but talking seemed to calm her a little.

"I'll check on you again soon," Riley said, motioning Candace to follow her from the room.

When they were out of hearing range, the supervisor gave her a quick rundown on the situation.

"We have one other patient who's nearly ready," Riley said. "Thank heavens it's her third, so she knows the drill."

"I take it this is Sue's first," Candace said.

"Yes, and the neighbor who brought her to the hospital had to leave for work once she was sure she was in good hands."

"She didn't come to any of my birthing classes," Candace said, suspecting that Sue wouldn't be quite so panicky if she had.

"A shame. I just hope her husband gets here soon."

"Do you want me to stay with her?"

"Please. See if you can calm her a bit. It's going to be a while before she's ready to deliver—probably not until this afternoon."

Candace found it unusually hard to go back to the young woman, but not because she lacked compassion. In fact, she deeply sympathized with the mother-to-be, knowing how hard it would have been to have either of her babies without Dean's loving support.

Lord, why did You take him away from me? No amount of praying and counseling had brought her an answer. No good could come from taking a father away from his children, from taking her beloved husband away from her.

She smiled when she went back into the labor room, but her heart wasn't in it. She forced good cheer into her voice. "And how are we doing here?"

Sue groaned as another contraction racked her body. Her light brown hair was plastered to her scalp, and her face was flushed and contorted with pain. "Does that answer your question?"

"We'll get through this, I promise. I know it doesn't seem like it now, but you're on the cusp of something wonderful." Candace gave the woman's hand an affirming squeeze. She began reviewing Sue's chart to get up to speed and resolved to get the woman's mind off her pain.

"Have you always lived in Slater?" Candace asked, knowing from experience that most people liked to talk about their hometown.

"I've lived all over," she said breathlessly. "I was an army brat and an only child. Wouldn't you know I'd marry a career soldier."

"You must have had a lot of interesting experiences," Candace said in a consoling voice. "Did you ever live in a foreign country?"

"Germany when I was in the sixth grade." Sue clutched the sheet with white knuckles but was temporarily distracted. "I wouldn't mind going back there when the baby is older, but it would be quite an ordeal traveling with diapers and all."

This wasn't the first time Candace had helped a patient through labor just by showing an interest in her. She was gratified that Sue was responding, relaxing a little as she waited for the next contraction.

Sue wrapped her arms across her chest and shuddered. "I'm cold."

Candace got one of the hospital's disposable blankets from a supply cupboard and arranged it over the patient.

"It looks like you're wrapping me in aluminum foil," Sue said with an attempt at humor.

"You can take it home when you go. It looks flimsy, but it's surprisingly warm if you ever go to football games."

She thought of sitting with Dean during the local high school games to support Dean's friend who was the coach. Why was everything reminding her of Dean this morning? She hadn't had a really bad episode in several weeks—the grief, always present, had been giving way to hope for the future since Candace had started her counseling sessions—but memories of him were especially poignant today.

She shivered at the memory. His death from a brain aneurysm nearly four years ago had been so sudden and unexpected that she'd been paralyzed with sorrow. Fortunately, her children gave her something to live for. With her mother's help, she was managing; but she still had days when life didn't seem complete without him.

They'd had a faith-based marriage and were raising their children to love and serve God. What had they done to deserve his early death? She'd prayed long and hard for an answer.

Candace shook her head to clear her thoughts and realized she hadn't been paying close attention to Sue's story about her husband learning he would be a father, but talking seemed to help the expectant mother. She stayed with her until Riley called her to another woman's delivery.

It was several hours before Candace could check on the young patient again. Her contractions were closer together, but Sue was remaining calmer between them. The LPN who had taken Candace's place looked happy to be relieved.

Candace tried her best to soothe her patient, much as she would have liked to take a short break. Her mind kept slipping back to her children. Had Howie remembered to take his mittens for recess? Would her mother remember to take Brooke to her orthodontist appointment after school? Her daughter would be twelve soon and was resisting the idea of braces. Candace hoped she wouldn't get tied up at the hospital and miss getting there in time to talk to the orthodontist.

"It won't be long now, Sue," Riley said from the doorway. "You're doing just fine."

"I want my husband to be here," Sue said, her voice quivering.

Fighting back tears, Candace remembered how much it had meant to her to have Dean by her side when both their children were born. She'd never seen him more excited than when he learned that both were healthy, beautiful babies. Seeing Sue, young and alone, go through labor without her husband had triggered memories that Candace usually reserved for the quiet hours of the night when she couldn't get to sleep.

Sue squealed loudly, bringing Candace to attention, but this time she wasn't crying out in pain. A young man in military dress bounded through the doorway and enveloped her in a hug.

Candace watched their happy reunion for a beat then stepped out of the room, relieved and happy for Sue. Another expectant mother had just arrived, and she left to give her full attention to the new admission.

It was past time for her break when Candace finally had a chance to go to lunch. Usually she ate in the hospital cafeteria; but on a whim she'd brought a sack lunch: a salad and one of the blueberry muffins her mother had baked for the kids' breakfast. After her hectic morning, it would feel good to sit in the staff lounge and relax.

She was about to enter the lounge when Penny Risser barged out of the room wearing her habitual scowl. Penny was only a couple of years older than Candace, but her brusque, disapproving personality made her seem middle-aged at thirty-nine. Some of the younger staff members had nicknamed her "The Dragon," since she guarded access to the hospital's CEO, Albert Varner. As his executive assistant, she usually kept herself aloof from other staff members, so Candace was surprised to see her leaving the lounge.

"Hi, Penny," Candace said in the most pleasant voice she could muster. "How are you today?"

"Too busy for chitchat," the woman said in her usual abrupt manner.

Candace watched her walk away, thinking it was a shame no one would tell her that olive green was the worst color she could wear. But unfortunately, Penny didn't seem to have any friends, and no one on the staff would risk her wrath to give fashion advice.

Going into the lounge, Candace reflected about the way some people used and abused important positions. She was thankful that harmony usually prevailed among the members of the nursing staff.

As soon as she opened the door, she was assailed by two familiar voices having a heated discussion. They stopped when they saw her, but she couldn't conceal her surprise. Of all the nurses in the hospital, Elena Rodriguez and James Bell were the least likely to have a disagreement. In fact, they often kept the staff entertained with their good-humored teasing.

"Candace, you got here just in time to referee," James said with a halfhearted grin.

"Oh dear, that doesn't sound good."

James was the only male nurse on the second floor and, having turned fifty-three a few days ago, one of the older ones. Tall and solidly built with graying hair and warm blue eyes, he set a good example for younger nurses, always calm and sympathetic to patients and helpful to other staff members.

"James is exaggerating," Elena said. "I just can't understand why Penny Risser thinks she can lord it over us."

Although Elena was in her midforties, she had the energy and spark of a teenager, always full of ideas and willing to do anything for her friends—one of whom was Candace.

"She has to keep Varner's confidences," James said in a reasonable voice. "After all, he is her boss."

"That doesn't make her my boss," Elena said heatedly. "It was just plain ridiculous of her to tell us that there's going to be a big announcement soon, then refuse to say what it involves. Maybe the hospital board is going to try to cut our salaries again—or even worse, lay people off."

"You don't know that," James said in a calm voice, even though his expression gave away his agitation.

"When is this big announcement coming?" Candace asked, sitting on the couch but momentarily forgetting about her lunch.

"Who can say?" Elena said. "Penny told us just enough to make me worry."

"Don't worry until there's something to worry about," James said philosophically.

"Maybe it won't affect us at all," Candace said hopefully, although she couldn't imagine why Penny would deliberately hint at something big if she wasn't supposed to talk about it.

"You sound just like my husband," Elena said, flashing one of her brilliant smiles. "Don't worry today about tomorrow."

Candace had thought more than once that Elena could have once been a fashion model with her long, slender body, lovely caramel skin, dark eyes, and lustrous dark brown hair. Fortunately, she loved her work in Intensive Care, and patients greatly appreciated her kind, efficient ways. It still warmed Candace's heart to know that Elena had recently renewed her relationship with God and was working hard to understand what the Bible had to teach. She often wished that her own faith was fresh and vibrant again, unaffected by her husband's death.

Just then, Anabelle Scott, a nurse supervisor in Cardiac Care, entered the lounge. At age sixty-three she was also one of the older nurses, and Candace valued her friendship. She was a kind, compassionate nurse, but she was also the voice of reason in the small group of friends.

"Ah, Anabelle, you're just the person we need," Elena immediately said, going on to explain Penny's veiled warning.

"It may have nothing to do with the nursing staff," James pointed out.

"Maybe Penny was only making herself sound important," Anabelle said. "Unfortunately, she does that sometimes."

"That sounds like playground nonsense," James said. "As in, 'I know something that you don't.'"

"Possibly," Elena said, sounding unconvinced.

"Anyway, we'll find out when Mr. Varner wants us to," Anabelle said. "We just had one pay-cut crisis. Let's pray it's not anything like that."

Elena nodded, but her expression remained grim. After a beat of silence, she said, "Back to work for me."

"Me too," James said. "Bye, you two." They headed down the hall together, Elena animatedly waving her hands as she reiterated her point to James.

Anabelle shook her head, then turned to Candace and said, "I didn't want to add fuel to the fire, but I've been hearing some rumors myself. What do you suppose our superiors have in store next?"

Candace sighed. "Who knows?" She didn't want to add Penny's vague warning to her list of worries.

That evening Candace debated whether or not to go to her grief counseling session, which had been rescheduled for tonight because their leader would be out of town on their regular night, Wednesday. She had initially started going at the urging of her mother several months ago and had made great strides since. But she still felt she should be ready to face the future without support from Lila and the others. Candace had become more a listener than a participant, not wanting to deprive others of their chance to express their sorrow.

Still, her counselor seemed very happy to have her continue. Lila Adams had opened her heart and her home to those in need of help. Not only was she a wise counselor, skillfully letting her patients work out their own solutions, but she brought together people who had a great deal in common. Candace counted several members of the group as friends, and she'd formed an especially close bond with Megan Gallagher, a widow who was struggling to come to terms with her loss. Sometimes, when the session didn't last too late, they went out for ice cream afterward. It helped to know someone who'd experienced the same kind of loss.

When she was assured that her children were happy and ready for bed, she decided that there was nothing to lose by going. It did do her good to feel part of the group.

The stately old homes on Lila's block were frosted with glistening crystals of snow, and the counselor's Queen Anne Victorian home reminded Candace of a birthday cake with its snow-covered roof and multiple chimneys sticking up like candles. She parked her black, compact SUV on the street. One of the group members was quite elderly, and Candace liked to save the parking spot in Lila's driveway for her on nights when the pavement was slippery.

Lila loved old things; but unlike many collectors, she used her antiques to create a warm and nurturing atmosphere. Candace let herself in, hung up her coat, and went to the closed door where the group sessions were held. The décor was a feast for the eyes; every time she went, she still found something new to admire. She especially admired a coffee table Lila had made from pieces found at salvage yards. It reminded her of the way the counselor helped people salvage their lives.

Megan wasn't here tonight. In fact, it was a very small gathering, no doubt due in part to the wintery weather. She knew Olive and Verla quite well, having heard their deepest sorrows and taken them into her heart. Lila soon came into the room with her usual plate of cookies.

Candace nibbled on a cookie as she listened to others' stories and challenges they'd encountered over the past week. As Olive cleared her throat to continue speaking, Candace sneaked a look at the clock.

"I've found a wonderful new way to console myself and commemorate my husband," she said. "I've been making a memory book of all the places we visited and things we did when we were traveling the country and selling my pottery."

"How lovely," Lila said, dressed tonight in sleek brown wool trousers that matched her hair and a beige cashmere sweater.

While Olive described her scrapbook, Candace thought of all the photos and memories she had randomly stored in boxes. Most were high up on closet shelves where her children never went. The idea of mounting all of Dean's pictures and souvenirs in one book that her children could enjoy was a good one. Maybe Brooke and Howie would benefit from a big project like this. When Dean first died, memories of him were too painful to relive; but now she felt she could take on a project like that.

"How did you feel as you were making the memory book?" Lila asked.

"I thought it would make me sad," Olive said, "but instead I remembered all the good times we had. It didn't make me miss my husband less, but I felt more and more thankful for all the wonderful experiences we shared."

Candace sat up a little straighter in her chair as she mulled the idea of a memory book.

As the session came to an end, the women chatted about the slick road conditions. Candace hadn't spoken much, but she took away the idea of doing something with all the photos that were haphazardly stored in different boxes and drawers around the house. Images of her husband and all that he'd accomplished in his too-short life deserved better treatment. Just that morning, Howie had been tearful over not knowing his father's face. With a resolved nod, Candace determined that Brooke and Howie needed to see what a vibrant and caring person their father had been.

Chapter Two

HARD PELLETS OF SLEET HIT THE WINDSHIELD AS Candace drove to work early the next day. She felt warm and snug in spite of the heater's weak performance. Brooke had sighed at her when she dug Dean's parka out of the closet, but there was nothing like a down-filled coat on a cold winter morning, even if she did have to fold up the sleeves to drive. She was grateful that she'd kept it when she gave the rest of his clothes to a charity on the advice of her counselor. Enveloped in his big coat, she felt warmth that had nothing to do with the temperature.

One good thing had happened the previous day. Brooke accepted her need for braces with far less angst than Candace had anticipated. Several of her friends were going to need them too, and it had become a status symbol among the preteens to have that first appointment with the orthodontist. Candace smiled to herself, musing on what a roller-coaster ride it was to have a lively sixth grader on her hands.

Only eight years old when her father died, Brooke had been emotionally fragile for several years afterward. For two months she hadn't spoken a word, and it had taken many counseling sessions before she began to come to terms with her overriding fear of death. Candace found dealing with typical mother-daughter issues a joy in comparison.

She drove down Fourth Avenue to Washington Street, which would take her directly to the hospital, but as she made the right turn, her eye caught a glimpse of bright pink on the passenger-side floor. Brooke must have dropped her winter hat after the visit to the orthodontist. It wasn't the only warm hat she could wear, but it was the only one she would wear. Candace smiled at her daughter's interpretation of fashion and checked her watch. Fortunately she was early this morning. She had time to take the hat home and still get to work before seven.

Candace made a turn at Third Avenue to backtrack to her house on the corner of Fourth and Dill and cautiously proceeded down the street. The haze of early dawn made visibility tricky, especially with wind-driven snow hitting the windshield. She could tell the pavement was slippery, so she slowed to a crawl when she saw a car parked just ahead. It turned out to be a big, old SUV with the back bumper hanging at an angle. She'd lived in the neighborhood long enough to know most of the families' cars, and this one she didn't recognize.

She pulled parallel to the vehicle and caught a glimpse of the interior, enough to see that there was a person huddled in the backseat, sitting upright with some kind of covering pulled up under her chin. It was almost surely a woman, and a fairly tall one at that.

"Something's wrong here," Candace murmured to herself, weighing her options.

The one thing she couldn't do was ignore the person in the parked car and drive on. She had a feeling the woman was in big trouble if she'd spent the night there.

Pulling to the curb in front of the old SUV, Candace left the motor running and the lights on. She was doing exactly what she'd told her children never to do: approach an unfamiliar vehicle. The person in the backseat hardly reacted as she came close. Something was very, very wrong here.

Candace tapped lightly on the back window, and the woman turned her head toward her.

"Are you all right?"

The figure made a vague movement that was probably a headshake. Candace tried the door but it was locked.

"Can you unlock the door?" she said loud enough to be heard through the glass.

For a few moments the woman didn't respond, then she very slowly moved one hand to pull up the little knob in the door that would release the lock. She was wearing what looked like threadbare cotton gardening gloves, and it took her several tries to get her fingers to work.

"Did you spend the night in your car?" Candace asked as soon as she opened the door.

The woman looked confused and disoriented, so Candace repeated her question and got a weak nod. Her trained eye immediately noted the woman's shivering, abnormally slow breathing, and lethargy. She was almost sure the woman was suffering from hypothermia—low body temperature that could lead to death if it wasn't treated.

Weighing her options, Candace quickly realized there was little she could do in the parked car. Hypothermia patients were fragile, and any attempt on her part to move the woman could have serious negative results. Jarring movement or vigorous handling could lead to cardiac arrest.

The blanket covering the slight figure was the so-called insulated weave, warm enough for an early fall evening but wholly inadequate for sleeping in a car in harsh winter conditions. She did the only thing she could, stripping off Dean's down parka and covering the woman.

"I'm going to call 911," she said. "I'm closing your door to keep the wind out. Just hang on."

Candace ran to her car, shivering in her scrubs. She'd worn a long-sleeved cotton turtleneck under the light cotton top, but the wind still cut through her like knife blades. She quickly found her cell phone in her purse and made the emergency call.

Her heater was still putting out a cozy flow of warmth, and she was tempted to huddle by it until the ambulance came. But the woman might need something from her, so she ran back to the old car. As rapidly as possible she opened and closed the back door and slipped in beside the hypothermia victim, gently putting her arms around her shoulders. She didn't know whether her body heat would help, but at least she could give the woman reassurance and human contact.

The car interior was as shabby as the outside was battered. All she could see were black plastic garbage bags—which might contain personal possessions—and the remains of a fast-food meal.

"The ambulance will be here in no time. We're only a few blocks from the hospital," Candace said.

The woman became agitated, her shoulders shaking under Candace's arm.

"No insurance," she managed to mumble.

"Don't worry about that or anything else," Candace said. "Hope Haven Hospital never turns away anyone in need. We'll work things out, but first you have to warm up."

"Afraid . . ."

"No, don't be. In the emergency room, they'll be very gentle with you. They'll do everything possible to make you comfortable. You'll be in the best possible hands."

Candace wasn't sure the woman comprehended what she was saying. But she still continued murmuring encouragement and reassuring her about the procedures to treat hypothermia. It broke her heart to feel how thin the woman's shaking shoulders were.

She glanced at her watch but couldn't remember exactly when she'd made the 911 call. It seemed like ages but probably was only a few minutes before she saw the flashing lights of the emergency vehicle.

"You'll be fine now," she crooned to the shivering woman. "These people will take good care of you."

Gus, one of her favorite emergency techs, opened the door as his partner, Vivian, rolled up the stretcher. Candace breathed a sigh of relief as the very competent pair took charge of removing the woman from the car, first handing back her down parka. She slipped into it gratefully, her teeth chattering from the cold.

There wasn't time to take the hat home to Brooke. She was already late for work. At least she could trust her mother to see that both children were adequately dressed for the weather.

She headed directly to the hospital, musing over the way she'd found the woman. If Brooke hadn't dropped her favorite hat, Candace wouldn't have headed back to the house, going down a street she never used on the way to work. How long would it have been before another passerby noticed the figure huddled in the backseat and stopped to investigate? Hypothermia could kill, and it was unseasonably cold, even for Illinois.

What kind of a world was it where a poor woman had to spend a winter night in her car?

Candace shivered, no longer finding warmth in Dean's parka.

James ate by himself in the hospital cafeteria so he could call Fern on his cell phone. She always told him he didn't have to check on her during his shift, but he countered by telling her that he liked hearing her voice in the middle of a hectic workday. His wife had been living with multiple sclerosis for most of their twenty years of marriage, and it made him heartsick to know that her symptoms weren't getting better. At least their two sons, Gideon and Nelson, were old enough to get themselves off to the middle school and high school without any supervision from their mother.

"Hi, sweetheart. I didn't wake you, did I?" he asked when the phone rang a little too long for his peace of mind.

"No, I was just resting a bit. I forgot to take the phone with me."

"Did Nelson remember to take his English essay to school?"

"I wasn't up when he left, but I don't see it on the kitchen counter. I should get up and see them off."

"No, they're big boys. It's good for them to take responsibility for themselves," James assured her. "Don't try to start anything for dinner. I'll stop at the grocery store on the way home and pick something up."

"You're so good to me. I hate it that you have to do your job and mine."

"I like taking care of you and the house. Love you, sweetheart."

"I love you too," Fern said in the voice she used when she was trying to conceal how weak she felt.

There was nothing he could do for her until he got home from work, but there was plenty to do on the second floor of the hospital. He hurried back to work, mulling over one particular patient. Millie, the only name they had for her, had been brought in suffering from hypothermia after a night in her car. By some odd stroke of fate, Candace was the one who found her and called 911. The patient's condition was poor after a night out in the cold, and routine tests revealed that she had uncontrolled diabetes. So far they knew nothing about her background or the circumstances that had left her homeless in a battered old vehicle.

Ordinarily a social worker would investigate her case and arrange for public assistance, but James felt that the severity of her illness demanded more immediate action. The medical staff needed information, but she'd barely spoken to anyone.

The new patient was alone in a double room with the curtains drawn across the window and around her bed. James approached quietly, not wanting to wake her if she was sleeping.

"Millie," he said gently, parting the curtain enough to see the patient.

She lay wide-eyed and motionless, an untouched lunch tray in front of her.

"Hospital food not so good today?" he said in a teasing voice.

Millie didn't react, a bad sign since patients usually loved to complain about the food.

"Hey, if you're not hungry, at least try a little juice. I see they've given you apple." He put a straw in the juice box, offering it to the patient. "You know, if you're going to get well, you need nourishment."

He held it up to her. She obediently took a couple of sips, then shook her head.

"The macaroni and cheese is actually pretty good," he said, spearing a morsel on a plastic fork and holding it to her mouth.

Again, she tried a bite but refused more.

"I know you ladies, always watching your weight," he joked. "Seriously, Millie, it would help us make you better if we knew a little more about you."

"There's nothing to tell," she said listlessly.

He'd seen the symptoms of despair and depression too many times in terminal patients, but something else seemed to be going on with Millie.

"Would you like to take a little nap before we talk some more?" he asked.

She nodded, and he took the tray of cold food away, leaving only the water. Maybe a healing sleep would be the best thing for her, although he knew she'd be disturbed many times today by technicians seeking answers to the poor state of her health.

The rest of his shift went by quickly, keeping him too busy to check on Millie again. Remembering his promise to bring something home for dinner, he left as soon as his replacement arrived and hurried to collect his coat. He was just leaving the building when Candace called out to him.

"James, wait a minute."

She was wearing a tan parka six sizes too big and walking gingerly on the heavily salted pavement in front of the hospital.

"Hi, Candace. Heading to your car? I don't think the staff parking lot will be salted this well."

Candace smiled. "I think I can make it. Actually, I wanted to ask you about the woman who spent the night in her car. How is she doing?"

"Not so good. They're only beginning to find out all the things wrong with her. For one thing, she has uncontrolled diabetes."

"Oh no."

"It's going to be a tough case. She won't even tell us her last name, let alone say anything about her health history. I tried turning on the old Bell charm and got nowhere." He laughed softly but without any real mirth.

"Can't believe that didn't work," Candace teased. "I know she's not my patient, but I sort of feel responsible for her."

"Maybe she'll talk to you. If you hadn't found her, there's no telling how long she would've been out in the cold."

Candace stopped walking and frowned pensively. "If she doesn't have anyone else . . ."

"It couldn't hurt to try," James said, wishing he'd thought of asking her to look in on the patient earlier in the day.

Candace looked at her wristwatch. "I think I'll go back and drop in on her. My family can get along without me for a few minutes more."

The door to Millie's room was open, and Candace could see her lying on the bed, her pale face surrounded by limp gray-brown hair. She looked even thinner and more fragile than she had in the backseat of the car, and she didn't react when Candace came up to the bed.

"Hello, Millie. Remember me? Candace Crenshaw."

"I told you, I don't have insurance to pay for this," Millie said in an accusing voice, gesturing at the room in general.

"That's the last thing you need to worry about," Candace said, gently touching the top of her bony hand.

"I'm not a charity case." Pride mingled with desperation in her voice.

"No one thinks of you that way. Hope Haven Hospital never turns anyone away. But they do need a little assistance from you if they're going to help you get better. Can you tell me what your last name is?"

"Of course I can, but I don't know whether I should. I won't be able to pay your bills, you know."

"This isn't about money, Millie. We need to know who you are and more about your medical history, whether you've had other health problems. The hospital staff can do wonderful things, but you need to be part of your own treatment."

"My last name is Lowell." She said it grudgingly.

"Do you have any family?" Candace felt like an intruder, but it was a terribly important question, considering that the patient had been living in her car.

"I had a brother—still do, as far as I know. But we had a falling out a long time ago. He tried to cheat me when our mother died, and I'd rather die than ask him for help." Millie closed her eyes and locked her thin lips together.

Candace took it as a sign that she wouldn't say anything else today. "I'm glad you're all warm and cozy. You don't need to worry about anything but getting better. If you don't mind, I'll come visit you again soon."

Millie didn't protest, and Candace had to accept that the visit was over.

Chapter Three

THURSDAY HAD BEEN A LONG DAY FOR ELENA. THE Intensive Care Unit was nearly full, and one patient in particular had required almost constant care. His liver was failing, and it had been her sad duty to keep his family informed. Every time she went to the visitors' room there were more people waiting for news and hoping to see him. She didn't expect him to be with them by tomorrow, but God worked in mysterious ways. She'd seen her share of miraculous recoveries. She wasn't about to give up on any patient.

She was fatigued and emotionally drained, but she still had to attend tonight's meeting of the hospital board. It was open to the public, and she planned to attend, whether Cesar thought she should be there or not.

She wouldn't have to pick up Isabel at preschool on her way home today. "Tito" would do it. Isabel smiled at the name her granddaughter had called Cesar when she was too young to pronounce *Abuelito*, a Spanish diminutive for grandfather. The name had stuck, even though Isabel would be going to kindergarten next fall.

In spite of her anxiety about the big hospital announcement, Elena cheered up as she pictured Izzy. She was a beautiful child with waist-length black curly hair and striking light gray eyes. She and her father, Rafael, had lived with Elena and Cesar since Izzy was an infant. When his girlfriend, Isabel's mother, deserted them shortly after giving birth, they had encouraged their son to live with them.

Oddly, Cesar was already home when Elena pulled into the driveway and under the carport of their ranch-style house. She was used to her husband's unusual hours, but it was still a surprise to find him home at this time of day. As a career policeman, he was more apt to work late than to get off early.

"Hello," she called out as she walked into the kitchen that was fragrant with the aroma of the chili in the Crock-Pot.

"Hi," Cesar said as he came into the kitchen.

"You're home early."

"Not exactly," he said in a weary voice that wasn't at all like him. He ran his hand over his face. "I guess I'll just come right out and say it."

A cold wave swept over Elena. "Say what?"

"I've been laid off."

Elena put her hand to her chest and took a deep breath. "Laid off?"

Cesar stared at the floor then out the kitchen window. "Yes, laid off. Not just me either. The bottom line is that there isn't enough money to pay the whole force."

"But you have seniority. Didn't the union protest?"

"They fought tooth and nail, but it's hard to argue against budget cuts."

Her heart ached for her husband. Not only was this a blow to his ego, but he would worry more than he already did about their finances.

"I'm so sorry," she said. "Maybe it's only a temporary layoff until the economy gets up and running again."

"Maybe," Cesar said, then flashed a weak smile. "So that was my day. How was yours?"

"Cesar—"

"I've had all afternoon to think on it, honey, and the last thing I want to do is think about it more. I don't think my mind can handle going over my options one more time. We'll weather this storm like we have all the others." He pulled her into a hug. "It's a good night to put on your robe and slippers and watch some TV."

She pulled back to look at him. "That sounds great, but I can't miss the hospital board meeting tonight. Penny Risser made a big deal out of how important the announcement will be. Even if she was exaggerating, I want to be there to put in my two cents if necessary."

"*Buela,*" he said, using her granddaughter's pet name for her, "do you really think the bigwigs will listen to you? Our union fought with all they had to stop the police layoffs, and here I am, along with too many other good officers."

"It's so unfair," she said, resting her head on his shoulder again.

"I'll drive you. The roads are starting to get slippery again."

"I'll be fine. The sand trucks will be out if it gets too bad."

"What's that saying? March comes in like a lion and goes out like a lamb. I've had enough roaring for one month." With a final squeeze, Cesar let go of Elena just as they heard the front door open.

"*Buela*, look what I made," Isabel said, coming into the kitchen holding out her latest project. "Daddy said he has to get gas but he'll be right home."

Elena smiled at the mop-haired hand puppet, the Styrofoam head covered with red yarn and the features drawn with bright colored felt pens.

"Isn't he handsome?" Elena said, glad to see that the unusual little figure brought a smile to Cesar's face.

"It's a she!" Isabel protested. "Can't you see she's wearing lipstick?"

"Yes, yes, I see that now."

Isabel truly enjoyed group activities. She loved playing with the other children and entered into all the offerings with enthusiasm. If the hospital board eliminated Elena's job or drastically cut her hours, there was no way they could afford to keep Isabel in preschool. She added this prospect to her list of worries and went into her room to freshen up for what could be an ordeal this evening.

She arrived shortly before the meeting was to begin, and there seemed to be an unusual amount of activity in the hospital reception area. It was scheduled for the conference room across from the CEO's office, but it was going to be crowded if all these people expected to fit into the room. Much to her surprise, she saw a camera crew from a TV station in a nearby town and a woman she recognized as a reporter from the local newspaper. Apparently Penny Risser was right about the importance of the announcement, but that did nothing to calm Elena's nerves. Big news wasn't necessarily good news.

She slipped into the conference room, the area dominated by a long table and comfortable chairs for the board members. Folding chairs had been set up wherever space allowed, and Elena found a seat in an inconspicuous corner. She'd just sat when, to her surprise, James came into the room. He spotted her and took the empty chair next to hers.

"I didn't expect to see you here," she said, grateful to see a familiar face.

"I had to take Nelson to a friend's house to work on a science project. As long as I was out, I thought I'd see what all the uproar's about."

The board members were taking their seats; and the hospital administrator, Albert Varner, was deep in conversation with the board president, Bernard Telford. The men couldn't have looked more different. Despite Varner's charismatic personality, his outward appearance was bland. In his late fifties, he still had dark hair with small traces of gray. His dark gray suit, light gray shirt and lavender-patterned tie looked as though they'd been designed to be worn together.

In sharp contrast, Telford was short and rotund with snow-white hair and a beard that reminded Elena of Santa Claus. He was wearing a yellow and green plaid sports coat that would have made a nice horse blanket and shapeless dark green trousers. Was this scruffy little man going to wreak havoc with her life by announcing another budget cut so soon after the big scare they'd recently had?

"Who's the tall man?" James asked in a quiet voice.

She turned her attention to the third man at the head of the table. He was tall and lanky with a long face and a lantern jaw. His thick salt-and-pepper hair was arranged in carefully styled waves. She didn't have a clue who he was.

"No one I've ever seen," she whispered.

"If this is just a budget meeting, why bring in an outsider?" James asked, a thoughtful expression on his face.

"Good question," Elena agreed. "And why is the press here? What could happen at Hope Haven that would warrant television coverage?"

"I guess we'll soon find out," James said, sitting up a little straighter on the chair.

Albert Varner took a seat to the left of the board chairman, so obviously he wasn't in charge of the meeting. Bernard Telford cleared his throat, then courteously requested that everyone quiet down.

"Ladies and gentlemen," he said. "We have an important announcement to all of us concerned with Hope Haven Hospital. First, though, I'd like to introduce you to Leonard Baxter, former member of the city council." He inclined his head to the stranger seated beside him.

"I've never heard of him," Elena whispered. "Not that I pay much attention to local politics."

"I think he was voted out after one term," James said in a low voice that only she could hear. "It was quite a while ago."

"Thank you, President Telford, and my thanks to board members Emmaline Palmer and Frederick Innisk for arranging this opportunity for me to speak to you folks." Mr. Baxter stopped for a few scattered handclaps and gestured for quiet, even though it wasn't necessary.

"First, I'm taking this opportunity to announce my candidacy for Bureau County Land Commissioner."

A photographer stepped directly in front of Elena, although she didn't know why a minor county job warranted so much attention. She didn't have a clue what a land commissioner did—or what it had to do with the hospital.

"Now for the big news you've all been waiting for," Mr. Baxter said with a small chuckle intended to sound modest. "Many years ago, the husband of Mrs. Frieda Jantz passed away in Hope Haven Hospital. Mrs. Jantz never forgot the kind and loving care he received from the staff. Last year she passed away at the age of ninety-eight after a lengthy stay in a nursing facility near her daughter's home in the Chicago area."

People in the packed room stirred restlessly, eager to learn where this was headed. Elena held her breath.

"Mrs. Jantz owned a large tract of land north of town, adjacent to the property line of Hope Haven Hospital. She has left this land to Hope Haven Hospital with no restrictions on its use."

The room buzzed as the spectators took in the implications of the announcement. Elena breathed normally for the first time since coming into the conference room. James smiled at her, and she grinned back, grateful that he was there to hear good news, not another threat of their livelihoods.

Baxter called on people who had questions about the gift, but Elena was too relieved to follow his answers. As soon as there was a lull, she quietly slipped out of the room followed by James.

"You were really worried, weren't you?" he asked as they walked back toward the reception area.

"Scared to death that there would be layoffs or cuts in our hours. I don't know what I would have done." Elena lowered her voice. "Cesar was laid off today because of city budget cuts, and we'll just be scraping by on my salary."

"The police force laid off officers?" James sounded alarmed. "Things must really be serious."

"I guess. Maybe the hospital will sell the land and give us all raises," she said optimistically.

"More likely they'll keep it for future expansion," James speculated.

"Either way, thank the Lord that it was good news." She felt her shoulders relax. After Cesar's announcement, she was glad she wouldn't have to bring more bad news home to her family.

Chapter Four

CANDACE CAME LATE TO THE STAFF PARTY, ALTHOUGH not by choice. Babies arrived in their own good time, and Charles Joshua Reynard Smith had been one of the stubborn ones. She smiled at the long string of names young Charley would carry with him for life, but she appreciated the use of family names. Her own son, Howie, was named after his paternal great-grandfather, a touching link to his father's side of the family.

The birthday girl, a Cardiac Care nurse whom Candace knew only casually, had just turned forty, an event her husband thought worthy of cake and fruit punch in the staff lounge. When Candace went into the lounge for a late lunch break, all that remained of the celebration was part of a chocolate sheet cake with white icing and a mound of sugary yellow roses.

She was pleased to see her three closest friends at the hospital lingering over their cake. Elena and James were having a heated discussion while Anabelle took dainty bites of the birthday treat and watched without comment.

"Candace, help yourself to some cake. You missed the singing and the punch, but this is one of the best sheet cakes I've ever tasted," Anabelle said, perhaps trying to interrupt the other two.

James tossed his empty paper plate into the trash can, but Elena was still holding her untasted portion.

"I've been trying to convince James that the hospital should sell the land and put the money into improving the level of care," Elena said. "Money has been so tight the last few years that there are all kinds of needs that haven't been met."

"It might be a bad decision down the road," James said in a calm, reasonable voice. "Someday, the hospital might need to expand. Parking is pretty tight already."

"They can build a parking garage," Elena argued. "Think of what it would mean to patients to update our technology. I bet you can think of new equipment the surgical wing badly needs. And some of the money could be invested so there's never a budget crisis like the last one."

When James didn't respond, she jabbed a plastic fork into her piece of cake and carried a bite to her mouth.

"Fortunately the decision isn't up to us," Anabelle said with a wry smile. "I imagine that the staff has many different opinions about what to do with the land."

"Well, I for one never want the hospital to be threatened again by a shortage of money," Elena said to the whole group.

Candace certainly agreed; but like Anabelle, she was sure the staff wouldn't have any say in the decision. She hated to see Elena upset about something none of them could control.

"You probably think I'm overreacting," Elena said, giving up on the cake and tossing plate and all into the plastic-lined receptacle. "Maybe I am, but I get so upset when I think of what the land could do for the hospital especially when our current needs are so urgent."

When the other three didn't seem inclined to continue the discussion, she shook her head ruefully and took a deep breath.

"Don't mind me. I've been on edge since Cesar told me he was laid off. If the town can make do with a skeleton force of police officers, what will happen to the hospital if there's another serious budget crunch?"

"I didn't know Cesar was laid off," Candace said with deep concern. "Surely there are other ways for the town to save money."

"You'd think so," Elena said in a weary voice that wasn't at all like her. "I guess we're such a law-abiding town that we don't need a big police force."

"It's only temporary, isn't it?" Anabelle asked, concern in her voice.

"We hope so," Elena agreed, "but meanwhile Cesar is beside himself with worry."

Candace put her arm around Elena's slender shoulders, trying to offer some solace but not sure what to say.

"Well, I have to get back to work," Anabelle said. "I guess we'll have to trust the hospital board to make the right decision."

Elena looked skeptical but joined Anabelle on her way out.

James smiled at Candace and shrugged his shoulders. "I guess I shouldn't have debated with her. After all, the staff probably won't have any say in the matter."

"It's good to talk things out," Candace said. "Elena will probably see both sides of the issue when she's not so worried about her husband."

"Let's hope so. Can I cut you a piece of cake?"

Candace shook her head but thanked him. She'd lost her appetite for a sweet treat.

"By the way, we still haven't learned much about our homeless patient," James said. "She's resisting the fact that she's diabetic, and we can't release her until she accepts responsibility for her treatment. It's thanks to you that she got help as soon as she did."

"I don't see how she'll manage without family or friends to help. She's rather young to go into an assisted-living facility."

"We have a whole staff of problem solvers," James said in a reassuring voice.

When her shift was over, Candace decided to make a quick visit to Millie. Maybe she needed a friend almost as much as she needed medical help. At least it couldn't hurt to look in on her.

Before she could act on her intention, she was called over to the nurses' station to take a phone call.

"Candace, honey, I just wanted to be sure you're coming right home after work," her mother said.

"What's wrong?" It wasn't like her mother to call her on the floor phone, but she knew Candace kept her cell phone in her purse while she was working.

"Nothing serious, I hope, but Howie's upset about something that happened at school. I picked him up early because the nurse said he wasn't feeling well. Now he's barricaded himself in his room and won't talk to me."

"I'll be right home," Candace promised.

She gathered up her coat—her own long wool one, not Dean's parka, and shrugged her way into it as she hurried to leave the building. Howie liked kindergarten. His teacher was a dear, an experienced teacher with grandchildren of her own. From what Candace could tell, she ran a friendly classroom where every child was special to her. She couldn't imagine what had happened to upset Howie so much that he wouldn't come out of his room to talk to Grammy.

Her mother met her at the door when she got home.

"It's just not like him to shut himself in his room and not talk to me," Janet said.

Her face, framed by silver hair, was crinkled in distress.

"I'm sure it's nothing you've done, Mom," Candace said, grateful once again that her mother had moved in with them after Dean's death.

Janet was a retired school media specialist with many years of elementary school experience. She adored all children, especially her grandchildren, and it was very unusual when she couldn't handle any situation that arose. When Candace and her older sister Susan were in middle school, their parents had divorced. Janet had raised the two of them with little help from their father, who'd moved to California and only rarely saw his daughters.

Candace threw off her coat and hurried up the stairs of the split-level house to Howie's closed door.

"Howie, honey, it's Mommy. Can I come in and talk to you?"

Although his door didn't have a lock, she'd always respected his right to privacy.

"Go 'way." His voice sounded teary.

"Guess what we had at the hospital today. A birthday cake."

"I don't care."

She wished that she'd thought to bring a little piece home to her son. He would've loved a big sugary rose.

"Grammy is planning meatloaf for dinner, your favorite," she said in a soothing voice. "Can I come in and see the papers you brought home from school today?"

He didn't protest, so she quietly slid the door open partway. Howie sat cross-legged in the middle of his bed, not playing with toys as he usually did. He was never inactive, so he must be very distressed.

Her heart melted at the sight of his coppery brown hair matted down from his winter hood and his green eyes scrunched up as though he was trying not to cry.

She did what any mother would: She sat on the bed beside him and put her arm around him, waiting until he was ready to talk.

"I hate school!" he said vehemently.

"You like your teacher," she gently reminded him.

"Yeah, but I still hate it."

"Do you want to tell me why?"

For a minute she thought he wouldn't answer, then he said with even greater anger, "Billy said a bad thing. He said Daddy didn't want to be with us anymore." Howie buried his face against her arm, and she could feel his shoulders shaking.

"Oh, sweetheart, that was a terrible thing for him to say, but you know it's not true. Daddy very much wanted to stay with us. Sometimes we just don't understand why bad things happen."

He sat up straight and sniffled, somewhat comforted if not completely convinced.

"Hey, Howie, there's something I want to show you. I think now is the perfect time."

"What is it?" he asked, rubbing his eyes on the back of his striped sleeve.

"Come into my bedroom. It's in there."

She took his moist hand and led him to the room she used to share with Dean. She couldn't answer his question about why his daddy had been taken from them, but she could reassure him about his father's love.

"Look here," she said, stooping to open the lowest drawer of her chest of drawers.

Under a pile of silk scarves that had once been her grandmother's, she found the blue velvet box that contained one of the treasures Dean had left behind. The Swiss watch had been his pride and joy, purchased at her insistence when he got a nice bonus at work one year. She sat on the floor beside the open drawer, and Howie joined her.

"When your daddy bought this watch, the first thing he said was that someday he wanted you to have it. It's one of the nicest things he owned, and when you're old enough to wear it and take care of it, it will be a gift from him."

She held it out and let Howie slip the large timepiece onto his small wrist. It was white gold with more functions than she'd ever figured out, but she could tell that her little boy was fascinated by the dials on the face of the watch.

"Look, you can tell what time it is in faraway places like Germany or Brazil," she said, pointing out one feature of the watch.

"China too?" Howie asked in wide-eyed amazement.

"Certainly China."

"Daddy said it would be mine someday?" He ran his finger over it, his voice touched with awe.

"Yes. That was why he thought it was worthwhile to invest in such a nice watch. If you take really good care of it, maybe someday you'll give it to your son." She swept Howie's hair from his forehead. "We'll leave it in my drawer for now," she said, "but if you ever want to be reminded of how much Daddy loved you, just ask me to see the watch. Never believe anyone who says Daddy didn't want to be with you."

The watch slid over his elbow as her son reached over to hug her. They made a little ceremony of returning it to the box.

"Now," she said, "let's see what Grammy has for an after-school snack. I'm in the mood for some apple slices myself."

With her family around her, bringing their troubles and joys to her, she felt loved and blessed. But the hardest time of the day was always bedtime. That evening when she got into the big cherry sleigh bed alone in the darkness of her room, she was overwhelmed by loneliness for Dean. This was the hour when they used to talk about the things that really concerned them.

Would she ever finish grieving? She was getting on with her life as best she could, more for her children's sake than her own, but she still missed Dean with every fiber of her being.

She couldn't get to sleep, even though she knew how early her day would begin the next morning. She thought back over everything she'd learned from Lila and through counseling, but nothing brought her enough peace tonight to doze off.

Her mind wandered to the memory book which she had been looking forward to starting, but now had reservations niggling at the back of her mind. Candace didn't know if it would help her or her children. It could be a painful process to backtrack over a loved one's life. Wouldn't every memory trigger a greater sense of loss? Was it even possible to capture the essence of her husband between the covers of a scrapbook?

She rolled restlessly onto her side, throwing her arm across Dean's side of the bed, unconsciously searching for his warmth. Instead she shivered at the coldness of the sheet and dragged the quilt under her chin. A memory book seemed to offer scant comfort in the dark of the night.

Chapter Five

Howie crawled into Candace's bed in his fuzzy blue pajamas a few minutes before her alarm was set to go off Monday morning. He complained of a tummy ache, but her motherly intuition—and a few questions—soon convinced her that it was a ploy to stay home from school.

It wasn't like her son to fake illness. On the contrary, he hated to miss school. When he'd had a runny nose and a cough back in December, she had to insist that he stay home.

"Do you think Billy will say more bad things if you go to school today?" she asked.

He was clutching his well-worn baby blanket, faded green with panda bears dancing across it, against his cheek, a habit he'd pretty much given up. She took it as a sign that he was still upset by what the other boy had said.

Howie didn't answer, but his silence gave her an answer.

"I could speak to your teacher and—"

"No!"

She smiled to herself. Her little boy had already learned that there were some problems he had to solve himself.

"I'll tell Billy that he eats worms and smells bad."

Candace had to stifle a chuckle. With as stern a face as she could muster, she told him that wouldn't be a good idea. As he ran his finger over the diamond design on the quilt, Candace continued. "Sometimes people say mean things just to get attention. It's best to ignore them, pretend you don't even hear them. Do you think you can do that?"

"I won't play with him at recess if he's not nice," Howie firmly decided.

Candace kissed the top of his tousled head and shooed him back into his own bed. She had to get up very soon, but maybe he would fall back to sleep. He went willingly, satisfied with his solution to the problem of Billy. She wished she could right what was wrong in her life so easily.

Before she went to work, she reached a decision. When she found Millie sleeping in her car, she'd been wearing a lightweight nylon jacket with arms so short they barely covered her wrists. The homeless woman was tall, considerably taller than Candace, with thin limbs but broad shoulders and an unhealthy mound of flesh around her middle. No matter what her eventual fate, she was going to need a warm winter coat.

It was time to give Dean's jacket to someone who badly needed it.

As much as the decision hurt, she put his last remaining garment into a plastic bag and took it with her to the hospital when she left for work. She hoped that Millie would never spend another winter night in her car, but no matter what harsh conditions she had to face, the down jacket would deliver on its promise of warmth.

Riley, the nurse supervisor, wasn't her usual cheerful self. She got to work after Candace—that in itself a bad sign—and by midmorning she admitted to having a severe headache, probably a sinus infection. Candace convinced her to go home, a decision made easier because the Birthing Unit wasn't at all busy. One mother had delivered in the middle of the night, a favorite time for babies, but the labor rooms were empty.

Candace had planned to see Millie during her lunch break, but with Riley gone, she felt it was her duty to stay on the floor. It turned out to be a wise decision. Shortly after noon, not one but two expectant mothers checked into the unit, one experiencing pains only seven minutes apart. The other, a young woman expecting her first, came in believing she would need a C-section, although Candace thought it was too soon to make that call.

For the rest of her shift, Candace was on the run. She liked being busy, but unfortunately for her and the rest of the staff, the second woman's doctor made life difficult for nurses who ventured an opinion. Candace could only be happy that he was semiretired with a small practice in a nearby town that didn't include many obstetric cases. He only came to Hope Haven a few times a year; but when he did, he expected everyone on the staff to answer to him. She suspected that at least some of his bluster was intended to mask his mediocre skills, but he was a holdover from an earlier age when nurses were subservient to doctors.

By the time her shift was over, neither mother had delivered, and she had a stress headache too. She did have to smile, though. She'd been worried about Howie's problem at school, and she'd had a "Billy" of her own to contend with.

She hadn't eaten since breakfast, and no doubt a snack would help her headache. She wanted to run home to her mother and enjoy some pampering, but she remembered Dean's jacket stuffed into her coat locker. If she was going to give it away, she wanted the deed done. Also, she wanted to see for herself how "her" homeless woman was doing.

Millie had a roommate when Candace went in to see her, but the woman in the other bed was snoring loudly, oblivious to what was happening.

"How are you feeling today?" Candace asked, her professional eye seeing a bit of color in the patient's cheeks.

"I should leave. I have to find a job and a place to live." There was desperation in her voice.

"Yes, I understand how eager you must be to get on with your life."

"The police towed my car away. Everything I own is in it."

"I'm sure your social worker will see that you get everything back."

"I can't do what they want me to, poke a needle into myself. I get dizzy just thinking about it. They say I'm diabetic, but I feel fine. There's nothing wrong with me that a job won't cure."

"I brought you something," Candace said, fearing that nothing she could say would comfort Millie.

No doubt the staff had tried reason and every other kind of persuasion in an effort to make her understand the seriousness of diabetes. But it was equally certain that she had to be able to manage the disease before she could be released from care.

"Here," Candace said, pulling Dean's parka from the bag. "This was my husband's. I'd like you to have it. I'm too short to wear it, but it should be just right for you."

"Doesn't he want it anymore?" Millie asked, not touching it even when Candace put it across her legs.

"My husband passed away. The jacket was practically new when he died, so I couldn't bring myself to pack it up for charity with his other things. But it's only going to waste hanging in a closet."

"It's so soft," Millie said, running her fingers over the stitching.

"It's down-filled. It will keep you warm even in subzero weather."

"Thank you so much," Millie said, her eyes moist with gratitude. "I've never had such a nice coat."

"I'm happy that you can use it."

"You've helped me so much. Will you tell the hospital people to let me go? I don't know where my clothes are or my car or anything."

"I can't do that," Candace said. "You need to trust the people who are taking care of you. They only want the best for you, and that has to begin with controlling your diabetes."

"Trust! How can I trust anyone? I worked at my job at the dry cleaners for nearly twenty-five years, ever since I graduated from high school. How could they tell me to go home and not come back? They said I wasn't up to doing the work anymore. Can you believe, they gave me one week's salary to last until I could find something else? And I paid my rent faithfully for all those years, but when my unemployment ran out and I got two months behind, the landlord said I had to leave right away if I wanted to take any of my things with me."

"I'm so sorry," Candace said, her heart aching for the woman in the bed.

"I prayed to God to help me find work," Millie said, shrugging her shoulders dejectedly. "We see how well that worked out."

She was weeping softly, and Candace couldn't find words to console her. She took her hand and gently squeezed it, sitting beside her until her crying subsided.

"I'm sorry," Millie said. "I just don't know what to do or where to go when they let me leave here."

"I'm sure you'll get all the help you need. Things will look up when you learn to manage your diabetes."

Candace wished she felt as confident as she sounded. As far as she knew, Millie had absolutely no one to look after her when she left the hospital. How desolate it would be not to have a loving family or dependable friends.

"I just feel lost," Millie said in a resigned voice that was more painful to hear than her crying. "My brother said he never wanted to see me again. He thinks I stole some of our mother's jewelry from him which couldn't be further from the truth. But I know how stubborn he is. He meant what he said about not wanting to see me. He doesn't care about me anymore. No one does."

Candace quietly struggled for a way to comfort her. Millie was spiritually lost, but she couldn't find the right words to reassure her about the Lord's love. The story of the lost sheep came to mind, but she felt helpless in the face of the patient's deep despair. Compared to Millie, she was greatly blessed with a family, a good home, and a career she loved. Still, Candace felt a close kinship to the patient, her sorrow, and her broken spirit.

"I'll come and see you again," Candace said. "Please, don't give up. Diabetic patients often have a hard time when they're first diagnosed. Hope Haven has a wonderful program to help you."

"I must seem terribly ungrateful." Millie sounded ashamed of herself.

"No, you're struggling with something really big. Things will work out. Let the staff here at Hope Haven help you. They understand what a tremendous change all this is. I have to go now, but I'll visit again soon."

"Thank you so much for the jacket." Millie managed a weak smile.

"It makes me happy to know you have it."

Candace felt drained as she walked down the corridor away from Millie's room. Giving away Dean's parka hadn't been as hard as she'd expected, but her inability to offer any kind of spiritual comfort had shaken her.

She rode the elevator down to the first floor, but she wasn't as eager to get home as she had been. She needed the busyness of family life, her mother's loving concern, and her children's reports of their day at school, but she wasn't quite ready to face all of them. First she needed to come to terms with her failure to offer Millie more than superficial help. The woman had cried out for spiritual guidance, and Candace had been found wanting.

Without making a conscious decision, she went to the open door of the hospital's small chapel. It had been some time since she'd sought solace there, and she wasn't sure that was what she wanted now. At least the room was empty, the light inside dim but not extinguished.

She took a seat at the back of the room, as far from the altar as she could. She didn't come to pray or to ask forgiveness for her failure with Millie. Rather, she needed the peace that she used to find there before Dean's death had changed everything.

Closing her eyes and breathing deeply, she tried to imagine all the prayers that had been offered up from this small chapel. The hum of countless pleas seemed to resonate around her, anxious relatives and friends praying for the recovery of loved ones, doctors and staff seeking strength and guidance, troubled people in need of the Lord's comfort.

One silent cry rose up, startling her with its power. She had thought it so many times before, and just when she thought she was on the verge of making peace with it in her heart, it cried out more ferociously than ever, refusing to be tucked away in her consciousness. *Why? Why Dean?*

Candace left quickly, desolate because there wasn't any comfort for her in the little chapel.

Her one goal was to get to her car as quickly as possible. She wasn't up to making small talk with anyone, let alone the woman who came up to the exit the same instant she did.

"My, you look as pale as milk," Penny Risser remarked, tossing the ends of a thick, hand-knit, yellow and green scarf around her neck.

The CEO's executive assistant reminded Candace of a garden gnome with her peaked red hat and bright green coat that made her look rotund. She was wearing rubber boots that looked like fisherman's footwear and thick wooly lamb gloves.

Candace couldn't hold back. She startled Penny and herself with an outburst of laughter, releasing the tension that had been building up all day.

"Did I say something funny?"

"Oh no, just a thought I had," Candace was quick to say.

"Are you all right?" Penny frowned, perhaps because she hated any situation that she couldn't control. "You really do look pale."

"No, I'm fine."

Candace held the door for Penny to go ahead of her, grateful that their cars were parked in opposite directions. It was all she could do not to break out in hysterical laughter, and she didn't want the officious executive assistant to know what she found so hilarious.

She stopped a moment to watch the garden gnome march away to her car. Any other time she would have sympathized with the woman's unfortunate taste in outerwear, but today it was just what she needed, comic relief in a day that had been relentlessly stressful.

Howie was waiting for her in the kitchen and snacking on orange slices when she got home.

"I ate Billy's cupcake," he excitedly told her before she had a chance to say a word.

Was this her son's idea of retribution? "Did you take it away from him?"

"No, he gave it to me."

"Was it because he was sorry for what he said?"

Howie frowned, thinking about it for a minute. "No, he wanted my choc'chip cookie."

"So you traded?"

"Yeah, but I took a bite of the cookie first."

He smiled so broadly she couldn't resist giving him a hug. *Sometimes*, she thought, *children can work things out better than adults*.

Chapter Six

JAMES FORCED HIMSELF TO FOCUS ON HIS JOB, BUT inside he was uneasy and conflicted. His courage and resolve hadn't been tested this much since his experience as a medic in the Gulf War. Reason told him that an invitation to speak at a conference was nothing like a life-and-death situation, but still, he was filled with dread at the prospect of public speaking.

He hadn't told Fern about the Wellness and Faith Conference, but he planned to the first chance he had to be alone with her when the boys were busy somewhere else. He'd been asked to give a presentation about the importance of nursing a patient's inner and outer needs, something he felt was extremely important. He was more than happy to share his experiences and thoughts on the topic. He was reminded of Matthew 26:41: "The Spirit is willing, but the body is weak."

James knew his weakness was his tongue, not his body. He simply didn't know whether he could talk in front of a group without reverting to the awful days of childhood when he couldn't speak a sentence without stuttering. He'd worked hard with a great deal of help from speech teachers to overcome his affliction, but he'd never completely lost his fear that it might return.

His early efforts at standing up in class and talking were still the stuff of nightmares. He vividly remembered giving a report on dandelions in third grade. He'd practiced at home until he knew it by heart, but when his name was called to present, he had difficulty with the first word of the report. He recalled looking at his classmates who started to look at each other and stifle laughter. He continued struggling until the teacher stopped him before he was finished to tell him that that was enough and he could sit down now. It was that incident that had earned him his nickname—J-J-J-James—which stuck all the way through high school.

After years of medical experience, he knew the roots of stuttering and why it happened—vowel sounds had been the particular bane of his young years. Some very understanding speech teachers put a great deal of effort into convincing him that stuttering didn't mean he wasn't intelligent.

He had many practical excuses for refusing the invitation, first of which was that he hated to leave his wife alone for the time it would take to travel to Kenosha, Wisconsin, attend the conference, give his speech, and return home. He knew the boys would take good care of her, and her parents lived nearby. The family had wonderful friends, neighbors, and church members who would look in on her and offer help. Still, he dreaded the possibility that she would have a bad episode of MS while he was gone.

When he did tell Fern about the invitation, she'd be adamant that he should go. She hadn't heard his stuttering, although he'd told her about it; but she would try to reassure him.

Of course, it would be hard to leave the boys too. They had so many activities requiring his support that he hated to go away for several days.

And if these weren't reasons enough for declining the invitation, he also had a lot of responsibility at the hospital. He took the welfare of every patient personally, and right now he was especially concerned about Millie, the diabetic who was in denial about her disease.

He supposed that these were valid reasons for not speaking at the conference, but faith-based nursing care was a cause close to his heart.

"James, you look like you have the weight of the world on your shoulders," one of the LPNs said to him at the nurses' station.

"Guess I've caught the blahs from these cold, gloomy days we're having," he said, trying to make light of his mood.

No matter how busy he was for the rest of the morning, he couldn't shake his anxiety about speaking to a large group. His stomach was growling before he focused on the need to take a lunch break.

The cafeteria was nearly empty, and he had to settle for what was left of the shepherd's pie, not a hardship because he liked the crusty mashed potato topping. He found a seat at a table for two, but he'd been too distracted to remember to bring a book to read, as was his habit when he ate alone. James loved the written word, and it was a hobby of his to continue building his vocabulary, perhaps as a holdover from the hard work of learning to control his stuttering.

He was halfway through his lunch when he looked up to see Anabelle taking the seat across from him.

"I don't often see you without a book," she said, setting her tea down on the table.

"Anabelle, hi. I didn't take the time to get one from my locker."

"You looked so lost in thought as though you have something serious on your mind," Anabelle said in a softly sympathetic voice. "Is there anything I can do to help out?"

He sighed then poked at the remainder of his shepherd's pie. "I have a decision to make. I've been invited to speak at a conference, and I'm not sure whether to accept."

"If you're concerned about leaving Fern and the boys, Cameron and I would be glad to have them stay with us while you're gone."

"That's really nice of you, but I think they'd be okay home alone for a few days. The problem is me, not them."

"What's the conference?"

It was so like Anabelle not to pry into the reason for his hesitation.

"It's the Wellness and Faith Conference. I'd be speaking about treating the whole patient from the standpoint of nursing."

"James, what a wonderful topic for you!"

"I guess," he said halfheartedly, "but I don't think I can do it."

She didn't ask why, but he found himself needing to tell someone about his apprehension.

"You've know me a long time," he tentatively began.

"Yes, I like to think we're good friends."

"The truth is, I don't think I can speak in front of a large group."

"I'm sorry."

He appreciated that she didn't launch into an argument to persuade him that he could, especially since she was the one who had taken over for him when he froze in front of the town council meeting.

"When I was a kid, I had a serious stuttering problem."

"No one would ever guess now."

"That's because I don't put myself into stressful situations that might trigger a relapse."

"And you think speaking at this conference might do that again?"

"Yes."

He was glad that she immediately understood his fear, but he was also afraid her opinion of him might be diminished.

"I can see you have serious concerns, but there's so much you could share with other health workers." She left her cup of tea untouched and rubbed her hands together.

"Or I could bomb completely and not speak a legible sentence." He smiled ruefully.

"What are the chances that you'd do a terrific job and put this worry behind you for good?" She massaged her right hand with her left.

He could only shrug.

"You could speak to a speech pathologist." Anabelle continued massaging her fingers while her gaze focused on him.

"Is something wrong with your hand?" he asked.

"Oh, it's just a little stiff. I just finished a quilt for the baby."

James smiled at Anabelle's obvious excitement for the arrival of her first grandchild due in just under two months.

"Now I'm making a quilt for Kirstie's bed," Anabelle continued. "Cameron says that I want to give her a little bit of home now that she's moved out on her own. I guess the two projects back-to-back added up to too much for my hands."

"It sounds like you have had busy fingers," James said, glad to talk about something besides his dilemma.

He knew that Anabelle had always been very protective of her younger daughter. When Kirstie was only ten, she'd had a bicycle accident that resulted in the amputation of one leg. Even though she was doing very well now as an elementary school teacher, her mother still worried about her the most of the three Scott children.

"Time to go back to work," Anabelle said, forgetting that she hadn't finished her tea. "And about speaking at the conference, you don't have to make a hasty decision. You live what you believe. That's a rare and precious attribute."

James rubbed the back of his neck. He'd worked with Anabelle when he first started at Hope Haven twenty years ago, and he respected her opinion a great deal. She hadn't said so outright, but she thought he should share his blend of faith and professionalism with others. He very much wanted to, but he didn't know whether he could.

Alone in her bedroom after dinner, Anabelle flexed her fingers, more annoyed than hurt by the pain in her right hand. No doubt she had overdone the hand quilting, although she really hadn't had time to do much lately. She didn't want Cameron to fuss over her, but she'd been hard put to stifle a gasp when she lifted a heavy casserole pan from the oven for dinner. When she exerted pressure on her hand, the pain seemed to radiate up to her wrist.

She didn't have time to worry about it. Genna Hamilton was picking her up for a special session of their quilting club. One of the member's aunts had given them a huge plastic bin of new remnants, an accumulation left from many years of sewing. They were all excited to plan what could be made from the bonanza. Their group was dedicated to making machine-sewn quilts for charity, and a new batch of material always excited their creative natures.

Anabelle had an idea to cut squares from all the flowered prints and design a garden pattern. Tonight's work session would be devoted to planning and cutting, so she went to her well-stocked sewing room and found her best scissors, the only tool she'd need.

Putting on her warm, green, quilted jacket and leather gloves, she waited by the front door until a car pulled into the driveway. Genevieve, or Genna as she preferred to be called, was Dr. Drew Hamilton's wife and a longtime friend of Anabelle's. Dr. Drew had cared for Kirstie after the terrible bike accident that claimed her leg. Genna had stepped in and helped with the rest of the Scott family during the crisis, and the two women had been fast friends ever since. Besides they were nearly the same age, and they shared a passion for quilting and for donating their work to charities.

Last year when Dr. Hamilton had suffered a heart attack, Anabelle had been able to give her friend moral support, although the couple's children were grown and no longer needed the kind of help Genna had given her.

Anabelle walked out to the car so her friend wouldn't have to risk the slippery surface of the walkway by coming to the door. No matter how often Cameron shoveled and spread a deicer, he couldn't keep up with the nasty conditions. She couldn't remember a year when March had started out quite this unpleasantly. Fortunately, he'd volunteered to walk Sarge, their new puppy, this evening. He was much more sure-footed, especially when he wore his heavy boots.

"Are you ready to design some gorgeous quilts?" Genna asked.

"Yes, I'm excited to see what we can do with all that new material."

Her hands were cold, and that made her right one ache even more. She didn't want to call attention to her problem, but she had doubts about using her scissors all evening. *Is this the onset of arthritis?* she thought. Like most nurses she knew, she tended to diagnose her own ailments. Next time she went to the pharmacy, she'd see what over-the-counter products might help.

The two women chatted about their families on the way to Dot Graham's house. The quilting guild would meet later in the month, but small groups often got together in homes to work on the charity quilts. They gave them to various service organizations, including one that assisted abused children. Anabelle had recently been investigating overseas relief agencies to see whether they could use warm quilts for refugees. So far she'd learned that they would have to be delivered to central locations before being shipped abroad, but the need was always great. Perhaps when she retired, she could devote more time and effort to expanding the guild's charitable work.

Several members of their small group had stayed away because of bad weather and a rash of colds and flu, so only a few women gathered at Dot's house that evening.

"I've been looking through our new material," their hostess said after serving hot tea and ladyfingers, "and I'm so excited. There's a wonderful assortment of colors, including my favorite blue. I think I'll do a log cabin design using mostly blues with touches of yellow and gold."

One of the youngest members of the quilting guild, Dot was still in her early thirties. She and her husband had one child, a raven-haired four-year-old girl with big brown eyes and a mischievous sense of humor. She sometimes hung out with the quilters, playing with scraps too tiny to be incorporated into a quilt, but tonight she'd gone to bed early with a slight fever and a cough.

"We nearly got through the winter without any sickness," Dot said. "It's unfortunate that so many of the children in preschool are sick now."

Anabelle enjoyed the casual conversation, catching up on what was happening in her friends' lives. In fact, she wanted to delay the time when they started cutting on the long board that protected Dot's dining room table during quilting sessions. She didn't want to make an issue of her sore hand, so the less time there was for cutting, the better.

"I've spread the new material out on the kitchen table," Dorothy said. "I know you're eager to see what we have. I'm thrilled with the variety."

The women, six in all this evening, filed out to the kitchen. They exclaimed over the huge amount of material and the great variety. Much of it was cotton, ideal for quilting. Because the donor had sewed for her children and grandchildren, there were many bright colors and complex patterns.

Anabelle was good at planning in her head, and she immediately saw that her idea of a flower-garden design would work well. Along with the others, she went through the remnants, choosing ones that would blend together beautifully.

"I can hardly wait to start cutting," Genna said, looking through the pile of material she'd selected.

Dorothy had provided pencils and big sheets of paper for those who wanted to work out their design and decide how many pieces they would need. Anabelle dawdled over hers until everyone else had taken a seat at the dining room table to start cutting. She'd made it a point not to rub her hand, but the cold had certainly revved up the pain level.

Her design was a simple one, just squares sewn together in strips, then joined. The charm would be in the way the different flower patterns blended together to look like a garden. Because she wanted as many different prints as possible, she was able to use some small bits of material that the others rejected.

She liked to use a cardboard pattern to ensure that all the squares were the same size. She worked slowly and carefully to make one, using some paper shears and large note cards Dot had available. At last she had to start cutting the material, or the evening would be a waste of time.

Of course, one of the really nice things about a quilting group was that they could visit and work at the same time. Anabelle started slowly, paying more attention to the conversation than her cutting. Her hand didn't feel too sore while she cut the first dozen or so squares, thanks mainly to her spring-loaded scissors that cut down on wrist and hand stress, but wasn't long before it began seriously aching just from the act of using it.

She went for more tea, offering to pour for the others. She held her fingers against the warm china of the pot for a minute or so, finding it soothing. Fortunately everyone was too busy working to notice. They would be sympathetic, of course, but she didn't want to call attention to her problem. It might go away in a day or so, and it wasn't as if she couldn't use her hand at all.

Genna needed to go home early that evening. One of her children was phoning, and she didn't want to miss the call. Anabelle bundled up her few cut squares and the rest of her material in a plastic bag Dot had thoughtfully provided, glad not to use her hand anymore that evening.

Once at home, she soaked in the bathtub, hoping the warm water would ease the pain in her hand. She wouldn't mention it to Cameron just yet. Pains usually got worse or went away on their own. She prayed for the latter. A problem with her right hand would interfere with much more in her busy life than just quilting.

Chapter Seven

By Friday afternoon, Candace's mood lifted as she looked forward to a weekend off work—grateful for the fact her supervisor had temporarily changed her schedule to give her Saturdays off instead of Thursdays. Maybe what she needed most was a time-out with no obligations to be anywhere. Even the sun was cooperating. It was still cold, but bright sunshine lifted her mood and that of her co-workers.

Before she could relax, she had to drive Brooke and a couple of friends to a birthday party, taking her turn at carpooling. They would get a ride home with another mother. Her daughter had been on pins and needles all week, planning what gift to take and what to wear. The birthday girl's parents had booked the indoor pool at the YMCA for the event, with pizza and cake to follow. Brooke could hardly wait to wear her new pink flowered bathing suit, ordered through the mail because local stores hadn't stocked swimwear this early in the spring.

Howie and Grammy had plans too. Mom was taking him on a mystery trip, something he'd enjoyed since he was two. This time it involved a trip to a store with a toy department and dinner at his favorite pizza place. He could easily guess where they were going, but he loved not knowing, unlike his sister who took great pleasure in anticipating an event.

Shortly after her shift ended, Candace went from house to house picking up her daughter and the other two girls. They bubbled over with excitement, and Candace was elated to hear Brooke enjoying herself so much.

"Have fun," Candace called after them as the three girls bounded out of the car and up to the door of the long tan brick building that housed the Y.

After a quick glance at the backseat to be sure none of them had left anything behind, she pulled away with a sense of freedom. She could do anything she wanted for the next few hours.

Maybe she would run a hot bubble bath, light a spicy scented candle, and soak until all the fatigue and tension of the week seeped away. It was a novel idea, since she usually only had time for a quick shower. Afterward, she imagined herself curled up on the couch with a good book and a big sandwich. How long had it been since she'd had time to read and relax?

As enticing as the vision was, she abruptly remembered what she'd left undone. She headed back the way she'd come, reluctantly parking her car in the hospital lot. Pampering would have to wait. She'd promised herself to keep an eye on Millie, and as far as Candace knew, she was still a patient in the hospital.

Candace could only imagine how lonely it was to be confined there with no visitors to break the monotony.

She wouldn't stay long, but she felt compelled to offer what comfort she could.

The corridor was largely deserted. Millie's door was open, and she immediately saw that her roommate had left. The bed curtains were thrown back, and the second bed was neatly made up with fresh sheets.

Millie sat in a chair by the window, staring out at the late afternoon sky. She still wore a cotton hospital gown and robe, a sign that she either didn't own replacements or her possessions were still in her car. Her gray-streaked hair was drawn back in a severe bun, and a book from the hospital library cart lay closed on her lap.

"Hi, Millie," Candace said from the doorway, not wanting to startle her.

"Oh, it's you."

Her voice sounded so sad that Candace's heart went out to her. It was hard enough being in the hospital, but it had to be awful when friends and family didn't come to visit.

"Candace, my name is Candace."

"Candace." She repeated the name with no inflection whatsoever.

"I just wanted to see how you're doing." She walked into the room and pulled up a chair to sit in front of Millie.

"I need to get out of here. I have to find a job."

"The sooner you get better, the sooner you'll be discharged," Candace said with more optimism than she felt.

"They made me give myself an insulin shot today." Her voice was a husky whisper that Candace had to strain to hear. "And I fainted. Passed out. All I remember is seeing tiny pin pricks of light, then nothing."

"That happens sometimes. It's hard to inject yourself."

Candace tried to console her, but the bottom line was that a diabetic had to learn to be responsible for treatment of the disease. Millie's condition must be serious if the doctor had bypassed oral medications and prescribed insulin shots.

"It will get easier," she reassured Millie, trying to sound positive.

"Doesn't matter. I don't have the money to buy insulin and test strips. I won't have until I find a job."

Candace saw the futility of trying to persuade Millie otherwise. If her social worker hadn't reassured her on that score, she wasn't likely to listen to her. She tried to think of something else to talk about. Dean had taught her that the one thing almost everybody liked to talk about was their hometown. "So did you grow up in Deerford?" she asked.

"No."

"Near here?" Conversation with Millie didn't exactly flow.

"You've probably never heard of it."

The more they played twenty questions, the more determined Candace was to break through Millie's reserve. "Was it in Illinois?"

"Yes, right on the Mississippi."

"Your parents' hometown?"

"My mother's. She took me and my brother there to live with my grandfather after my father left us."

If Millie's life was a jigsaw puzzle, this could be an important piece, though she still hadn't given her any information she could use to trace family members. The vacant expression in Millie's watery blue eyes wasn't encouraging.

"What's that you have on top of the book?" Candace asked, noticing a slip of what appeared to be newsprint.

"One of the nurses gave it to me."

Candace remembered seeing the small story about a woman being found in her car and admitted to the hospital.

Millie rolled the bit of paper between her fingers. "I feel so humiliated, being found like that."

Were all Millie's memories bad? Candace struggled for a way to help her remember happier times.

"What was living by the Mississippi River like? I'm always in awe of it when I cross one of the bridges. It's hard to imagine it starting with a shallow stream in Minnesota and ending as a great river in New Orleans. My husband and I wanted to take one of those paddle wheelers they run for tourists, see the whole length of the river, but we never had a chance to do it before he passed away."

"I did that once." Millie got a faraway look in her eyes. "My grandfather took me from Illinois to Louisiana on his river barge. He was the captain." Her voice perked up enough to encourage more questions.

"What a wonderful experience." Candace was genuinely impressed.

"My mother didn't want me to go. I can still hear them arguing about it. She thought I was too young, and the river men were too rough. I was only eight, but Grandpa wanted to take me before he retired. He was already pretty old by then."

"Do you know what they hauled on the barge?"

"Whatever they could get, I guess. All I remember are big brown bags. Could have been grain. I only had eyes for the river." Millie got the faraway look again, as though she were seeing the broad expanse of the Mississippi in her mind.

"And how long did it take to get all the way downriver?"

"Oh dear, I don't remember." A ghost of a smile fleetingly softened the sharp features of her face. "I was just a kid. But I do know it took us longer than the newer barges. We ate a lot of fish that the men caught. I didn't like it at first, but I learned to eat whatever was available. Being on the river all day made a person powerful hungry."

Millie sat up a bit. "Grandpa told me a lot about the old Mississippi. He said a person's life was like the river. It started with a trickle at the headwater and broadened as you experienced more of life. He showed me how men tried to control the river. You know, with locks and dams and floodways to help with the flooding, but the river has a spirit of its own. It meanders and changes channels. It can be hurt by nature and by man, but treated right, it nourishes people and wildlife. My grandpa knew the name of every bird in the wetlands. I wish I could remember everything he taught me."

Millie's entire demeanor had completely changed. Her eyes sparkled, and her thin lips formed a wistful smile. Candace had tapped into those happy memories she knew Millie had to have somewhere. She wanted even more to do something to help turn her life around.

"You know, Millie, the river of your life is still flowing," she said, hoping she didn't sound patronizing.

Millie's sharp little laugh was startling after the nostalgic memories she'd just shared.

"I've run aground on a sandbar, and I don't see any way of getting off." She slumped down in the chair, and her voice was tinged with bitterness again.

"Things have a way of working out," Candace said, frustrated with herself because she didn't have more to offer. "Sometimes the Lord works in mysterious ways."

"Sometimes He ignores people. My mother raised us to be church people. She got after us if we didn't learn our Sunday school lessons, but I never did sort out what God wanted from what Mama wanted. Praying didn't work out any better for me than asking my mother for help."

Candace felt heartsick, unable to find words of faith to console Millie. Her own trust in the Lord was being severely tested. She still couldn't understand why Dean was taken away from her, and she didn't know how to convince the homeless woman that God would take care of her.

"I'm so sorry." Her heart ached for Millie, but she didn't know what else to say.

"Don't be. You're kind to come see me. I haven't talked about Grandpa and the river for a long time. You know, sometimes when the river gets blocked up, the water opens up a new channel. The flow has to go somewhere. Maybe there's a reason why I lost my job and my home. I just can't see it right now."

"Maybe when your health problems are under control, you'll see things differently." Candace felt more qualified to give her hope on that score.

"Maybe." Millie didn't sound convinced.

"I'll come back again." It was the only promise she could make.

The house was quiet when Candace got home. Much as she loved her family and looked forward to seeing them every day, she was glad for a little time alone. She couldn't stop thinking about the river as a metaphor for life.

She went to her room and picked up a framed picture of Dean as he'd looked shortly after they met. He was a handsome man, warm and caring; and she wondered what advice he would give if he could talk to her again. Would he like the idea of life as a river? Perhaps he'd see their union as the confluence of two fast-flowing streams, greater together than separately.

She kicked off her shoes and sat on the bed, pulling up her knees to rest her chin. In her mind she could see patches of the Mississippi glimpsed from the shoreline and from bridges she'd crossed. The great river had never failed to awe her, and slowly she began to realize that it held a message for her. Millie was right. Life was, in many ways, like a broad river that sometimes meandered and other times rushed by with destructive force. At its best, it created wetlands that nourished life, but the river's gifts didn't come without hazards.

Was it an accident that she'd dropped her papers one windy day in college, and Dean had stopped to help? Did God send the wind because they were meant to be together, or was it only a quirk of fate?

Her mind wandered to the memory book. Maybe it would help put their love and her loss in perspective. If nothing else, it would help Brooke and Howie remember their father.

She was so motivated that she went to the calendar hanging in the kitchen to see when she could begin the journey backward. The first place to go was the campus where they'd met. She scanned the squares on the calendar and came to a conclusion. There was no time like the present. If Mom agreed to watch the kids, Candace would begin tomorrow. The roads were clear of ice and snow, and there was the prospect of sunny weather all weekend. She'd begin at the University of Illinois campus in Chicago.

Would making the memory book bring contentment or more pain? She was trembling, but she was committed. She wanted to revisit every precious moment with Dean.

Chapter Eight

CANDACE WAS PACKING HER CAMERA IN A TOTE when Brooke came and stood quietly in the bedroom doorway. Although it was early for her to be up on a Saturday morning—just past seven—Brooke was dressed in jeans and a bright blue sweater with her long blonde curls neatly brushed.

"Grammy said it's okay if you have one friend come over today," Candace said, feeling a bit guilty about leaving her children on a weekend. "But just one."

"I don't want anyone to come over."

"Oh? Do you have something planned for the day?"

"I want to come with you."

Candace hadn't expected this. Brooke wasn't fond of long car drives, and she probably would be bored visiting places in Chicago that had little meaning for her.

"I want to help," her daughter said earnestly.

Candace debated with herself before answering. Would a day spent retracing her early days with Dean upset Brooke, or would she benefit by being part of it? This was one time when her daughter might be a better judge of what was best for her.

"If you're sure you want to come, I'd love to have you." She walked over and gave her daughter a brief hug. "We'll be doing a lot of walking, and it will be really cold near Lake Michigan. Be sure to wear plenty of warm clothes and your snow boots."

"I thought you'd say no." Brooke smiled broadly. "Howie is too young to come, isn't he?"

"Yes, it will just be the two of us. Have a bowl of cereal so you don't have to ride on an empty stomach. We'll leave as soon as you've had breakfast."

"Mom, I already had toaster waffles. I can be ready in two minutes—maybe even one."

Candace smiled as she watched her daughter rush away. A mother-daughter outing wasn't part of her plan, but she loved the idea of showing Brooke the campus at the University of Illinois in Chicago and visiting with her the places that had special meaning. Part of the idea behind the memory book was to share it with her children. It had been over three years since Dean's death from a sudden brain aneurysm. Perhaps Brooke's memories of her father were getting dim, and she needed to be reminded of the vibrant, loving person he had been.

By the time Candace gathered her things together and put on warm winter outerwear, Brooke had bundled up and was waiting by the door with her backpack.

"I put in some granola bars and a bottle of water for each of us," Brooke said. "Do you think we need sandwiches too?"

"No, we'll have lunch at a nice restaurant, but it's good you thought of a snack."

She smiled, remembering the elaborate preparations her daughter had made for yesterday's birthday party. With Brooke, getting ready was half the fun.

Candace wasn't crazy about driving on the complicated system of freeways that would take her to the Chicago campus, but at least the roads were free of ice and not as busy as they were on weekdays. Brooke studied the atlas her mother always carried in the car and was surprisingly good at spotting exits and entrances. By the time they got to the outskirts of the city, she was doing a competent job of navigating, especially considering that she wasn't quite twelve.

Candace had worried that the trip would be a sad one, bringing all her grief to the surface again, but sharing it with Brooke made it seem more like a pleasure outing. To keep her own mood positive, she thought of all the good things in her life. Her children were a blessing beyond compare, and without her mother, she would flounder at the difficult job of being a single parent and a full-time nurse.

Hope Haven was a wonderful place to work, in spite of occasional setbacks and problems. The staff was encouraged to treat the whole person, offering compassion along with competent care. She wouldn't trade the friends she had there for any others. She shared a bond with people like Anabelle, James, and Elena because they all cared deeply about the patients who came there for help.

And then there was Heath Carlson. The radiologist technician was her age, and like her, he'd suffered a devastating loss. When he was only twenty-three, his fiancée had been killed by a drunk driver. She knew that they could never be more than casual acquaintances until she confronted her family's grief, but it still warmed her heart to know that a kind, pleasant man sought her friendship. Maybe she would go bird-watching with him this spring, a hobby he often mentioned.

"Don't you think so, Mommy?"

Candace realized that she hadn't been listening, and she was a bit surprised to be called "Mommy." Brooke was rushing toward adulthood, and part of her progress was to use the more formal "Mother."

"What was that, sweetheart?"

"I knew you weren't listening," Brooke accused her. "I can always tell when you get that faraway look."

"I'm sorry. I was just thinking about some people at the hospital."

"I said maybe we should look for a really beautiful scrapbook while we're in Chicago, one nicer than we could find in Deerford. I want Daddy's memory book to be special."

"It will be, sweetheart. I promise."

The campus was near a major expressway interchange called the Circle, and Candace had to give her full attention to being in the correct lane at the right time. If she missed an off-ramp, she'd have a hard time getting back to where she wanted to be. It was her biggest fear when it came to driving on multiple-lane highways. After the quiet streets of Deerford, the traffic in the big city was nerve-racking. She had to be constantly alert for drivers who raced from lane to lane and cut off slower vehicles like hers.

Brooke was intimidated by the fast-moving traffic and no longer tried to navigate. Candace remembered that Dean had always insisted on driving when they entered or left Chicago. It was a responsibility she'd happily turned over to him, but she couldn't think about that now.

The campus spread out from the East Campus near Lake Michigan where Dean had taken courses for his business degree to the West Campus where the Medical Center was the focus for her nurse's training. Her mother had teased her about the prospect of meeting a doctor, dentist, or pharmacist in the huge health services complex; but once Janet met Dean, she loved him like the son she didn't have.

"Are you up for a lot of walking?" Candace asked.

"Oh, Mother." Her tone said that she could do anything her mother could.

"There's a parking structure on Halsted Street. I think I'll leave the car there. If you get too tired, we can always get a cab to bring us back here."

She was trying hard to think of nostalgic places to visit, and at the same time, keep her daughter entertained. She knew what Brooke would like best: walking on a sandy Lake Michigan beach, something she and Dean had especially enjoyed when they were still students. Candace shivered at the thought of the frigid air beside the huge inland lake and decided not to mention it unless the day warmed up.

"Are we just going to walk around all day?" Brooke asked as they strolled down one of the wide walkways on the campus.

She could see it through her daughter's eyes. The Chicago branch of the university had been designed in the 1960s, and the buildings, as large and impressive as they were, didn't hold much appeal for a child.

"There's where Daddy and I met," she said, pointing at a snowy strip of open ground. "Of course, then the grass was green."

"You told me about the wind and the papers and all that stuff," Brooke said.

"So I did." She wistfully recalled the moment, wishing she could rewind time and be standing in this very spot all those years ago. With a small sigh, she shook her head to clear her thoughts and turned her attention back to Brooke. "Why don't you walk over there a little ways, and I'll take your picture?"

"Why don't I take your picture?" Brooke asked in a reasonable voice. "I wasn't there when you met Daddy."

"All right." Candace took off her gloves to get the camera out of its case and handed it to Brooke. "You look through here and . . ."

"Mother, I know how."

"Sure you do."

"Now smile," Brooke said when she had the camera ready to shoot. "I don't want a picture of you looking sad."

Candace did her best to comply, but she was surprised when Brooke broke out in laughter after snapping the photo.

"Did I look that silly?"

"The building behind you looked like a great big hat on your head. Can I take a better one?"

"One more, then I want to take one of you. It will be a new memory for us, the time we came to Chicago together."

Now that she was here, Candace started to remember all the places that held memories. She and Dean had studied together in the library and at the hospital. He'd insisted on walking her home even when she worked a late shift. One snowy January day, they'd had a snowball fight that left them both soaking wet and howling with laughter.

His friends became hers, and her friends became his. He had a great gift for bringing people into his circle, while she was quieter and content with a handful of close friends.

What could she possibly show their daughter that would suggest the heady experience of being truly in love for the first time? Brooke was still too young to understand how the right person could change life forever, but she did love her daddy with all her heart. As they walked, Candace pointed out places where Dean had had classes and where the two had spent time together, believing that their lives would be perfect because God had given them each other.

She could see that Brooke's interest was rapidly waning, especially when they ducked into the library for a brief look.

"You sure had to walk a lot when you were in college," her daughter said.

"Yes, we did."

In fact, she and Dean loved to walk together, sometimes going down to the beaches of Lake Michigan or walking to the city center. They were so much in love that they were scarcely bothered by sharp winter winds or gusty rain. Dean's first Christmas present to her had been an amazingly soft cashmere scarf that reminded her of the blue water of the lake. It had made her feel warm on the most frigid days. She still had it tucked away, wrapped in tissue as a priceless reminder of their long walks.

Brooke scuffed her feet restlessly as they left the library, and again her daughter inadvertently brought home a truth. Her best memories of Dean weren't tucked away in buildings or rooms. She remembered walking arm in arm or holding hands, using their valuable spare time to be together. They talked endlessly about their plans for the future, sharing their most secret thoughts and aspirations. It was as if their love was so great that it couldn't be contained inside.

She felt the pain of his loss acutely at that moment, but she was also comforted by the memory. She couldn't bring back the euphoria of their early days together, but she could gather their experiences together in a memory book and relive them when she felt lonely and forsaken.

"Can we go see the doll house?" Brooke asked as they walked toward the huge health services complex on the West Campus.

It took Candace a moment to realize what she was asking. "You must mean the Fairy Castle at the Museum of Science and Industry."

"Yes, you and Daddy took me there when I was little. I used to lie in bed and think what it would be like to be tiny and live in a beautiful palace like that. Daddy told me a movie star had it made and gave it to the museum. I really would like to see it again."

Candace hadn't even thought of going to a museum while she was driving the two and a half hours to Chicago, but it suddenly seemed like a wonderful idea. Brooke had memories of her father too, and it was touching to know that she remembered the trip to see actress Colleen Moore's famous Fairy Castle. She couldn't have been older than six, yet she hadn't forgotten her daddy's taking her there.

"We'll do it," Candace said decisively, discounting the inconvenience of reclaiming her car and driving there.

Brooke squealed with excitement and practically ran back to the parking garage.

Candace was always a little intimidated by the massive interior of the Museum of Science and Industry. She'd come here as a child and as an adult, and her feelings had always been the same: There was so much to see and do that it was overwhelming. Today, though, the focus of the visit was clear. Brooke needed and wanted to see the wonderful thing that her father had shown her.

The movie star's famous castle was on the lower level, and Candace was happy to see that the line to circle around it wasn't particularly long. Except for one Girl Scout troop, there weren't any large groups of children. The museum was a popular destination for school and other field trips, but they were fortunate that it wasn't nearly as crowded as it sometimes was.

Brooke was literally dancing with excitement as they waited for their turn, standing on tiptoes in an attempt to see over those in line ahead of them. Candace could hear a swoosh of air escape from her lungs when they got close enough to see the fantastic eight-foot-tall castle.

"Daddy held me on his shoulders," she said breathlessly. "I'd never seen anything so pretty."

Even though Candace had seen the castle several times before, she was as enchanted and awed as her daughter. The chandelier was made with real diamonds, emeralds, and pearls. The kitchen with the copper stove was modeled after the one from the story of Hansel and Gretel, and there was a round table similar to King Arthur's.

Brooke quickly spotted tiny details like Cinderella's glass slipper and tiny golden plates, knives, and forks. She listened with rapt attention to the little organ in the chapel that played soft music and puzzled over the polar bear rug with tiny teeth in the prince's bedroom.

Candace enjoyed her daughter's pleasure even more than the delights of the castle, although she'd never seen anything to rival the graceful floating staircase. But of all the wonders in front of them, she was most touched by a weeping willow in the garden. It cried real tears that fell into a miniature pool, reminding her again of the river of life and her quest for healing. She turned her head away so Brooke wouldn't see the moisture in her eyes, but her daughter was too enchanted by the sights in front of her to notice.

They had to move on so others could see the castle, but Candace shared her daughter's reluctance to leave it.

"I have an idea," she said as Brooke shuffled away. "Let's go to the gift shop and see if they have a book about the castle. That way you can enjoy it again and again in your memory."

They were able to buy a copy of Colleen Moore's own book about the castle, and Brooke clutched it against her as if it were a great treasure.

"How does lunch sound to you?" Candace asked. "It's a long ride home."

They went to the Brain Food Court where Brooke took her time choosing between pizza and a thick deli sandwich. Candace opted for a tossed salad, but ended up eating a good share of her daughter's pizza. Brooke was too interested in her new book to pay much attention to food.

On the way home, Brooke gave up on being the navigator and kept her eyes glued to the pages of the lavishly illustrated book as though she were memorizing every tiny detail.

"This was such a good day, Mommy. Do you think Daddy saw how much fun we were having?"

"I wouldn't be surprised, sweetheart." Her throat was tight with emotion. She was so very happy that Brooke had shared this first step in creating the memory book.

Chapter Nine

JAMES SMILED TO HIMSELF AS HE WATCHED FERN sitting on her special kitchen stool and cutting out biscuits with a round cookie cutter. She had a magic touch with them, and they'd please the boys, who didn't count omelets among their favorite dinners. It was terribly important to his wife that she was able to participate in their dinner preparations.

"Biscuits and honey," he said, giving her an encouraging pat on the back. "I can't think of anything I'd rather eat."

"I like having breakfast for dinner once in a while," said. "Sometimes you have to eat something just because it tastes good."

"I agree. Everyone needs some comfort food."

He gave silent thanks to God that his beloved wife was doing better after a severe relapse some months ago. She was ten years younger than him, and the pink sweatshirt she was wearing with jeans reminded him of their early days together when she'd had enough energy to run circles around him. In his eyes, she was still as pretty as when they'd married twenty years ago. She was petite, barely five foot, with wavy brown hair cut in a pixie style and brown eyes lively with love in spite of the cruel symptoms of MS. She'd been diagnosed nearly eight years ago, and the ups and downs of the disease could have broken a stronger spirit than hers.

James put the pan of biscuits in the oven and asked his wife to move from the counter to the kitchen table so he could sit across from her.

"There's something I want to share with you while the boys are still outside," he said.

"Oh dear, that sounds serious."

He'd considered not telling her, but now that Anabelle knew, it didn't seem fair to leave her out.

"Nothing bad," he quickly said. "Just a decision I have to make."

"Now you've made me curious." She hung her cane on the back of an empty chair and gave him her full attention.

He pursed his lips, considering how to begin.

"I've been invited to speak at a Wellness and Faith Conference on treating the whole patient."

"James, that's perfect for you! It sounds like a wonderful opportunity to share your ideas on Christian caregiving."

"I knew you'd say that," he said with a small smile.

"Of course. Who could possibly do a better job?"

"I don't think I can do it, Fern. Public speaking just isn't my thing," he said, shaking his head.

"James, you'd do a wonderful job. Where is this conference?"

"Wisconsin, but—"

"Don't say it! You don't want to leave me alone with the boys, but that's no reason to refuse. You know I'd have plenty of help while you were gone. Mom would be over here every day checking up on me. And I've been feeling stronger lately."

"I don't want to leave you, but that isn't the reason I have to decline. The real problem is my stuttering. I don't know whether I can get through a presentation without a relapse." James avoided his wife's gaze.

"Sweetheart, in all the time I've known you, you haven't had a single incident. You handle stress better than anyone I know." She placed her hand on his. "Look at all the scares I've given you, and you've been a rock. The doctors at the hospital trust you completely. You've never buckled under any kind of pressure." It was a long speech for her, and she sank back against her chair looking tired.

"This is different." He'd known it would be difficult to explain to his wife and biggest supporter.

"I know what you're going to say. You're going to tell me it's like a phobia. Some people can't get on elevators, and you can't speak in public. But I'm not buying it. When the moment comes to stand up and do it, your faith will carry you through. I'm sure of it."

"I wish I had your confidence," he said, reaching across the table and taking her hand in his.

"Just tell me you haven't turned it down yet," she said in a soft voice.

"No, I haven't, but—"

"When do you have to let them know?"

"I have a few weeks."

"Promise me that you'll at least give it more thought. This is a wonderful opportunity."

"I'll think about it," he reluctantly agreed.

"Whatever you decide, I'll support your decision," she said, giving his hand an encouraging squeeze. "I want you to do it for your own spiritual growth, not to please me."

"What would I do without you?" he asked, standing and planting a light kiss on her forehead.

"You'd probably burn the biscuits," she said with her wonderful gift for keeping him focused. "How about calling the boys so they have time to wash up before dinner?"

Sunday morning was sunny and dry but still cold enough to keep the snow from melting on lawns and fields. At least the roads and walkways were free of ice, a blessing since it meant Fern could go to church without needing her wheelchair. It was a long walk from handicapped parking to the church entrance for a person using a walker, but she much preferred to enter the church standing upright.

James walked beside her, his heart swelling with gratitude for this small improvement in her health. He knew there was no cure for MS, but each small sign of remission was a gift from God.

Their two sons had run off to sit with their friends, but James didn't mind this show of independence. To him, the morning was glorious because Fern was with him.

They were early, deliberately so to give Fern plenty of time to get to a pew, but this morning they were stopped several times on their way. Since the newspaper and television coverage, people were curious about what the hospital would do with the large tract of land gifted to Hope Haven. He had to admit that some of the rumors he'd been hearing were making him nervous—a drag-racing track near the hospital would be disastrous.

"I have no idea," James said to two elderly members of the congregation in answer to their question.

The white-haired woman chatted with Fern for a minute or so, but her husband didn't seem to believe that James didn't have a clue about what the administration would do with the generous gift. Unlike Elena, whose opinion he usually valued, he accepted that there wasn't much he could do about it. He doubted that riling up the staff and getting people to sign petitions would have any influence on the board's decision.

Their own church, the Church of the Good Shepherd, had been the recipient of a large parcel of land adjacent to the brick worship center, one of the oldest in town. Many members of the congregation had urged that it be sold to make needed repairs, including work on the sharply slanted roof. Instead the church council had used the land to create a large grassy recreation area with facilities for picnics, a basketball court, a ball diamond, a volleyball court, and two small playgrounds for little kids. It was the center of congregational life in the summer. Their boys spent a great deal of time there, making them feel more a part of the church. If the hospital put the land to good use as the church had, James would be pleased.

The organ called them to worship, and James helped settle Fern in their usual spot. It amused him that most members were creatures of habit, the two of them included, sitting in the same pew Sunday after Sunday. In fact, he was in high spirits until he started to think of giving a talk in Wisconsin.

What was holding him back from accepting? Was it pride? Fear? He had to admit it was a little of both, but also didn't want the caregivers at the conference to focus on his stutter instead of the message.

He looked forward to their minister's sermon every Sunday, but this morning it was the church member reading the selection from the New Testament who really captured his attention. Cameron Scott, Anabelle's husband, came to the front to read Luke 21:1–4.

"As he looked up, Jesus saw the rich putting their gifts into the temple treasury. He also saw a poor widow put in two very small copper coins. 'I tell you the truth,' he said, 'this poor widow has put in more than all the others. All these people gave their gifts out of their wealth; but she out of her poverty put in all she had to live on.'"

James loved the message of the widow's gift, but today he was struck by something else. Cameron had a strong, pleasing voice. He read with conviction, and there was utter silence in the church as people gave him their full attention. For a brief moment, James envied Cameron's confidence and the ability to project his voice. Then he reminded himself to be grateful for all the gifts the Lord had given him, even if public speaking wasn't one of them.

After the service, Fern stayed in the pew to visit with friends who came to talk to her. Her social life was limited, and she enjoyed visiting with other women. James drifted away, giving her time for "girl talk," but he would return soon to walk her to the car. She tired easily and usually took a long nap on Sunday afternoons.

He saw Anabelle standing by a table near the entrance where people left fabric for the charity quilts her group made. She was putting the donations in a big canvas bag, talking to another woman of the congregation as she did it.

James hung back a minute until the other woman left Anabelle alone. He wanted to say a word about how well Cameron had read.

"James, it's so nice to see Fern getting to church without a wheelchair," she said when he approached.

"We take it day by day," he said, "but lately she's been a little better. I don't see Cameron. I wanted to tell him how well he read today."

"He went to get the car, but I'll be sure to tell him you said so. Have you given any more thought to speaking at the conference?"

"It's been on my mind quite a bit," he said with a sheepish grin. "If I had a voice like Cameron's, it would be a no-brainer."

"You have a very pleasing voice," Anabelle was quick to say.

"Thanks, but it's not necessarily reliable."

"James Bell, you're over fifty years old. If you don't give it a try now, you may never know what you're capable of doing," she scolded in a kind voice.

He knew she was speaking out of friendship, but she hadn't known him before his stuttering was under control. His own parents had found it painful to hear him struggling to bring words out, although they gave him as much support as they could.

Shaking his head, he remembered how it felt to have words locked inside of him. He'd never really conquered his fear of ridicule—one of the joys of graduating high school was leaving J-J-J-James behind—and he was sure no one could understand how fragile his hold on normal speech was.

"I have an idea," Anabelle said, an earnest expression in her big brown eyes. "Why don't you practice by reading in church?"

"No, I couldn't possibly."

He'd done a lot of jobs for the church, from lawn mowing to serving on committees, but he'd never even thought of volunteering to read.

She lifted up the glasses that she wore on a chain around her neck and gave him a searching look.

"How do you know if you've never tried?"

"If I start stuttering—"

"Even if you do, the people here won't think the worst of you. In fact, most would admire you for trying."

"You want me to practice for something I don't want to do by doing something else I don't want to do?"

She laughed at his awkward phrasing which was all the more comical because he loved words and had a more than adequate vocabulary.

"Exactly," she said laughing. "Cameron is in charge of scheduling people to read. He can find a time very soon. He always tells people well ahead what to practice reading. It's the perfect opportunity for you to try out your public speaking skills."

"You're assuming I have some," he said morosely.

"You're the scoutmaster of Nelson's troop. Certainly you have to get up and talk in front of a group for that."

"Yes, but I suppose I just feel more confident in that role. Talking to the kids is different than talking to my peers."

"Think it over. You don't have to agree this minute."

James knew what would happen if he took time to decide. He would fret and stew, and Fern would be sure to pick up on his mood. She would try to persuade him to read, and he'd end up doing it to please her. He very much wanted to say no, but he always found it hard to refuse a fellow Christian, especially one as committed as Anabelle.

"Okay." He just managed to get the word out.

"Okay, meaning you'll think about it or you'll do it?"

"Okay, I'll do it, but be sure Cameron doesn't give me verses with unpronounceable names." His mind wandered to names in the book of Numbers. He wasn't sure how he'd pronounce Manasseh, Ishvite, Kohathite, and Shuthelah.

Anabelle grinned with pleasure. "You'll do beautifully, and you'll wonder why you were ever hesitant."

As he and Anabelle parted, he muttered, "Shuthelah" under his breath.

James shrugged his shoulders in the gray and blue plaid sports coat that served as his church outfit in winter. "Shuthelah," he said again.

He'd rather work a double shift in surgery than even think about walking up to the front of the church and reading out loud. What would Gideon and Nelson think if their father stuttered too much to finish the reading? They didn't know about the problem that had caused him so much misery when he was young. Would they be embarrassed for his sake? Would their friends tease them about their inarticulate father?

Chapter Ten

ELENA SAT AT HER SEWING MACHINE STARING AT the ruffled yellow dress she was making as Isabel's Easter outfit. She loved making pretty clothes for her granddaughter, and a quiet Sunday afternoon was the perfect opportunity to sew. Rafael had taken his daughter with him to visit a friend, and Cesar was engrossed in a basketball game on TV. There was nothing to distract her from her latest project.

Unfortunately, she was having problems. Lining the sheer material with matching nylon cloth was more difficult than she'd expected, and the sleeves, in particular, were giving her fits. Who knew the pattern for a child's dress could be so complicated?

Her sewing skills were up to it, she knew, but she couldn't seem to concentrate on the slippery pieces of cloth. After a frustrating half hour, she put aside the partially completed garment and turned off her sewing machine for the day. She had three weeks until Easter, so she would try again when she didn't have so much else on her mind.

She thought again about the major worries in her life: Cesar's unhappiness about losing his job, and just what the politician who'd come to the hospital board meeting was up to. Was he hoping to somehow influence who acquired the land? Would he favor friends of his over what was best for the community?

She'd seen his campaign ad in the paper. Leonard Baxter made it sound as if he'd personally donated the land. Not only that, he was talking up the possibility of developing it, but he avoided specific details. Elena was all in favor of selling the land to make improvements in the hospital, but what she didn't know about the board's plans bothered her. She'd heard the possibility of a strip mall being floated. And could the board truly be considering allowing a drag-racing track to be built? The very dynamic of the community was in jeopardy.

"No one is going to let me run the world," she reminded herself out loud, although she earnestly believed it was important to take a stand on things that mattered.

She followed the drone of the TV, deciding to begin reading a library book while her husband watched his game. The curtains in the living room were drawn because Cesar didn't like a glare on the screen while he watched sports. It took her a moment to realize that her husband was sound asleep in his recliner, oblivious to the action on the television.

Elena smiled down on her handsome husband, loving the way the years seemed to fall away when he was sleeping. They'd both been tense since he was laid off his police job, but they were trying hard not to snap at each other. Cesar had had trouble sleeping at night, so a nap was the best possible thing for him.

She walked over to the TV and turned it off, intending to leave the room so she wouldn't wake him.

"Hey, I'm watching the game," he grumbled.

"You were sound asleep," she teased.

"I just closed my eyes for a minute."

"Then tell me what the score is."

"Okay, I guess I slept a few minutes," he admitted. "I may have to get used to sleeping days again."

Elena remembered his days as a rookie cop when he'd worked the late night shift, but this was the first she'd heard about a return to that kind of schedule.

"Do you mean you've been called back to work, and you didn't tell me?" She didn't know whether to be angry or happy.

"No such luck. I didn't want to get your hopes up, but it's hard for me not to tell you things. It's been on my conscience all weekend. I have a job interview tomorrow."

"That's wonderful! Why wait until now to tell me?" she asked.

"You're not going to like it much if I do get the job."

"Cesar, you know I'll support you, no matter what you decide to do."

"They need a guard at the monument company," he said.

"Why? I mean, all those big chunks of granite. What is there to guard?"

"They had some expensive vandalism last summer. I don't have all the details, but it has to do with their insurance. A young college guy has the job now, but he wants to quit. I'm afraid it doesn't pay much," he said apologetically.

"Something is better than nothing," she said, trying to sound upbeat.

"I don't have the job yet." He sounded stoic.

"How could they possibly not hire you?" Elena said, crossing her arms. "A real cop?"

"They might think I won't stay long enough to make it worth hiring me." Cesar picked at a hangnail.

"Then we'll just have to pray they recognize what a fine employee you'll be."

"How about making a snack for your fine husband? We haven't shared a big bowl of buttered popcorn since I don't know when."

"Yes, we should celebrate your job interview no matter how it comes out," she said, pleased that Cesar sounded more cheerful than he had since he'd been laid off.

When she got Howie to bed Sunday evening, Candace found herself alone in the house. Her mother was enjoying an evening out with some of her longtime friends, retired teachers who liked to get together at each other's houses for supper and a visit. Brooke was working on a homework project at Dawn's house and would get a ride home from her friend's mother.

The house was quiet, too quiet. At rare moments like this, Candace longed to talk to Dean about all the little things that had happened during the week. He'd had a way of putting things into perspective, making the ups and downs of her life seem like minor speed bumps.

She wanted to hear his voice so badly that he seemed to be speaking in her head. She heard a soft murmur of approval for the way she was taking care of the children and doing her job, then it faded away.

Pacing through the dimly lit rooms on the main floor, she tried to remember the sound of his voice. Although she would recognize it in an instant if she could only hear it, she couldn't summon his deep, masculine tone. When he'd laughed, it came from deep in his throat. The thought of it made her feel terribly alone, but she couldn't call it up in her mind. Was this part of Dean fading from her consciousness? She felt a stab of panic that any part of him should recede from her memory.

To occupy herself in the empty house, she went to the kitchen and pulled out her recipe file. The kids always loved her peanut butter cookies, so she found the recipe and sat staring at it.

It wasn't Howie and Brooke who couldn't get enough peanut butter cookies. They'd been Dean's favorite, and she'd baked them often in the early days of their marriage. A big wet tear landed on the recipe card, and she knew she'd never bake them again.

But Dean's love of the cookies gave her another good memory and reminded her of the book she was making with Brooke. Yesterday they'd looked seemingly all over Chicago until they found a scrapbook worthy of dedicating to him. They'd set up a card table in the living room so they could work on it anytime without interfering with table space needed for meals or homework.

She went to it now, turning on a floor lamp to illuminate the impressive leather-covered scrapbook sitting open on the table. Brooke had picked the color, a rich forest green, without realizing that it was her father's favorite color. The large pages were archive paper, safe for the most precious photographs and souvenirs of his life. Brooke had lined up the materials they'd need to assemble it: two kinds of scissors including one that cut in a fancy pattern, glue, a medicine cup to hold small amounts of it, toothpicks, and a package of decorative papers.

Together they'd made a list of many things to include. There was a large box of photographs to sort through, and she still had to go to the drugstore to pick up the ones they'd taken in Chicago. Dean had been a pack rat, accumulating all kinds of odds and ends in his desk and dresser. She'd avoided sorting through them after the painful process of bagging his clothes for charity, but now was the time to do it. She had no idea what she'd find, but the search was sure to trigger more memories.

She opened the scrapbook to the first page, a pristine white space to hold mementos of their too-short time together. She didn't know where to begin. How could she stick feelings on paper? What could she put it the book that would even begin to reflect the love she had for Dean?

Candace sat in front of the open book for a long time, and eventually her thoughts centered on Millie. The woman had so little cause for joy in her life that Candace felt guilty for the depth of her mourning. Was it worse to have known great happiness and lost it or never to have experienced it? She knew the answer. She wouldn't give up a single moment of her time with Dean. Now she had to learn to live with memories but go on with her life.

The image of a river spoke to her again. Her life seemed like a leaky barge, limping downriver to the ocean, but for the sake of her children, she had to learn to navigate past the shoals and sandbars.

The doorbell rang, startling her off the folding chair beside the table. Brooke was home, and she'd forgotten to unlock the front door. Even though she carried a house key, her daughter liked to call attention to her arrival with a noisy chorus of dings.

"Mom, I thought you'd fallen asleep," she said, noisily dropping her backpack on the floor and shrugging out of her coat.

"No, I'm wide awake. How did the project go?"

"Okay, I guess. We're making a chart about the food groups, and all we did was cut pictures out of her mom's old magazines. What did you do?"

"Put Howie to bed. I thought of making cookies, but I didn't."

"That's okay. Grammy made a whole batch of chocolate chip yesterday."

"I did find a recipe for peanut butter cookies—your father's favorite. I thought we could put it in the memory book."

"Is it all sticky like some of your recipes?" Brooke asked.

"I suppose it is."

"Well, maybe we can recopy it. We want Dad's memory book to be perfect."

"That's a good idea."

Candace wanted to encourage Brooke's participation as much as possible, but she remembered Dean reading the list of ingredients loud as she mixed them. Should the memory book be a work of art, a memorial to him, or should it contain all the fragments that had meaning in their life together? There had to be a compromise somewhere, but for now, she was gratified that their daughter wanted to be part of it.

"Dawn's mother wanted to know all about the land left to the hospital, like I'd know because you work there," Brooke said heading toward the kitchen. "She owns that candy shop on Main Street, and all the store owners are worried. They think the hospital will sell the land for a mall, and no one will shop downtown anymore. Is that true?"

"It's only a rumor, as far as I know," Candace said, unable to offer any real information.

"I hope so. Dawn said her parents might have to move if the candy store goes bankrupt. That would be so terrible. We've been friends forever."

"I wouldn't worry about it yet. It's much too soon for any decision to be made."

She was glad that Brooke had given her something to think about besides how much she missed Dean. She needed to live in the here and now. If the memory book helped her focus on the things that were important to her family and the hospital, it would be the best thing that could happen.

"Time for bed," she mildly suggested.

"Oh, Mother, I'm not a baby like Howie. I don't need a hundred hours of sleep every night."

Candace smiled to herself. Her little girl was growing up, but bedtime was bedtime.

"If you want a snack, get it now. Then it's up to bed for you."

"Is Grammy home?"

"Not yet, but you don't need to wait up for her."

Brooke had been battling over bedtime since she was two. Tonight Candace was up for the challenge. With any luck, Brooke might turn out her light in a half hour or so.

"I was hoping we could paste things on the first page of Dad's book."

"Good try," Candace said, concealing a grin.

She hugged her daughter without giving her a reason. There was nothing like a bedtime struggle to keep a mother grounded in the here and now.

Chapter Eleven

JAMES COULDN'T HELP STARING DOWN AT THE FACE on the gurney as he pushed the young girl toward a bed in the recovery unit of the surgical suite. She was still under from the anesthesia, and her face was deathly pale except for dark smudges under her eyes. He knew that she was nineteen, but she looked younger than his fourteen-year-old son Nelson.

The victim of a terrible traffic accident, the young girl—Ginny was her name—would live, but she faced months of agonizing rehab. Even then, it was likely that she would need further surgery on her crushed leg. Perhaps she'd never walk again without an orthopedic appliance.

He murmured a prayer for her healing, and he prayed especially that she had the faith and strength to believe in her own recovery.

The driver of the car—her boyfriend, according to her parents—had fared even worse. He'd been airlifted to a Chicago hospital with such severe injuries that he had less than a fifty-fifty chance of surviving. As a father, James wanted to pound his fists in frustration. Neither had been wearing seat belts, and the young man's reckless driving had caused the death of an innocent man in the other car.

Without being asked, the nurse in charge of recovery helped James move the patient onto the bed, positioning the leg encased in bandages. His responsibility ended here, but he lingered at the bedside for a few moments. Nothing about his job disturbed him more than to see a young person senselessly maimed. What had been in that boy's head when he recklessly risked his girlfriend's and his own life, not to mention that of a complete stranger?

His son Gideon was already driving with a special permit that allowed him to take his mother places when necessary. Soon Nelson would be eligible to start learning too. What could he say or do to keep them from tossing away their lives by showing off behind the wheel? He believed that they were both sensible boys, not inclined to be disobedient or foolish, but an accident like this forced him to face his own helplessness as a parent. He could teach, and he could pray for their safety. At times like this, it didn't seem like enough to protect them from themselves.

Giving himself a mental shake, he left the room. His faith had wavered when Fern was diagnosed with MS, but he knew that the Lord had given them both the strength and courage to face it. He believed with all his heart that his life and his family's were in God's hands.

He had a pang of conscience when he remembered how reluctant he was to testify to his faith at the upcoming wellness conference. For a brief moment, he thought of Apostle Paul's missionary journeys and the unnamed affliction that hadn't kept him from doing the Lord's work. Then his pager went off and James got too busy to think of anything but the tasks at hand.

It was one thing for Candace to tuck in her children for the night, but quite another to persuade her mother that it was time to go to bed. Janet was always in a talkative mood after an evening with old friends, and last night they'd visited until her mother's eyes were visibly drooping. Candace often had trouble getting to sleep, and this morning she felt as though she'd only snatched a few hours of rest before her alarm clock rang.

Her shift started off with a frenzy of activity in the Birthing Unit. One mother-to-be had seemingly invited everyone she'd ever known to be present when she delivered. Her husband couldn't even get close enough to hold her hand as aunts, cousins, sisters, friends, and the two prospective grandmothers crowded around her, most of them offering advice or recalling their own birthing experiences. Candace and Riley had to use an inordinate amount of time and all their persuasive powers to thin out the crowd, which even included a girl of no more than thirteen or fourteen who'd taken off from school to be there.

The birth was still hours away, and members of the support group kept sneaking back "just to see how things are going." Riley even mentioned calling security to prevent the mother-in-law from hovering over the increasingly uncomfortable patient and talking nonstop about everyone she'd ever known who'd had a difficult delivery.

"When did having a baby become a spectator sport?" Riley complained to Candace. She tucked a blonde lock into her usually perfect french twist and smiled ruefully.

"I can take lunch later if you need me here," Candace offered.

"No, go while the going is good. I don't want my best nurse collapsing from hunger."

"Like that would happen! But thanks. I am hungry. I'll get back as soon as I can."

Candace remembered her promise to take a short break as she walked into the cafeteria. She settled for a cup of tomato soup and a grilled cheese sandwich and sat alone to eat. She was so intent on finishing quickly that for a few moments she didn't realize that someone was standing beside her table.

"You know, nurses are allowed time to chew their food."

She looked up into Heath Carlson's smiling face, his vivid blue eyes looking down at her bland lunch.

"I can tell you don't work in the Birthing Unit," she teased the radiologist tech.

"Do you mind?" He gestured at the empty chair across from her.

"Of course not. I haven't seen you in a while. I mean, have you been sick or something?"

She didn't want him to think that she kept track of his movements. She liked him a lot, but being friends with an unmarried man was different from her casual friendship with a happily wed man like James.

He put his cup of coffee on the table and sat down.

"I went to a conference in Boston. I didn't learn much, but I enjoyed so much East Coast seafood that I'll have to double my workouts to make up for it. What did you do on your weekend off?"

"Brooke and I went to Chicago, to the university and the Museum of Science and Industry. She was enchanted by Colleen Moore's Fairy Castle."

"Sounds like a fun day out."

"It was actually for our memory book that we're making about Dean." Her voice faltered. She didn't know whether Heath really wanted to hear about her grief therapy. He'd gone through so much after his fiancée was killed by a drunk driver. She didn't want to remind him of his own pain, but she needn't have worried.

"That's a wonderful idea. I was never into making scrapbooks, but it helped me to gather all our mementos and put them in a special carved wooden box. I used to go through it often. Now it just comforts me to know that it's on the closet shelf if I need it," he said.

With anyone else, the conversation might have gotten awkward, but Candace didn't feel that way with Heath. He was so understanding that she always felt good after listening to him.

"It's always nice talking to you," she said, happy that she could say that without implying anything more than friendship. Maybe someday—but she wasn't ready to think about it yet.

"I feel the same way."

She'd forgotten to finish her sandwich, but she felt a sudden urgency to get back to the Birthing Unit. She didn't know whether it was a new baby calling to her, or she just wasn't ready to carry the conversation with Heath any further.

"Have to get back to work," she said, making a show of checking her watch.

"Yeah, me too. Funny how breaks go so much faster than working time." He grinned and stood up, then remembered his coffee and hurriedly drank the rest.

"See you later," Candace said as she hurried away.

Would he take that as an invitation? Why was it so hard to say exactly the right thing to Heath?

By the time Candace's shift ended, the mother with the big audience still hadn't delivered. Maybe her baby wanted to stay hidden from the crowd of curious well-wishers. It was a fanciful thought, but Candace was so tired she was practically sleep-walking.

She nearly bumped into James as she went into the locker room to get her coat and purse.

"You first," he said with exaggerated gallantry that brought a smile to her face.

He didn't return her smile. It wasn't like James to look so morose. He began pulling on his heavy leather driving gloves. He didn't ask about her family, which was odd. He was usually warm and friendly, always interested in the welfare of others.

Candace shrugged into her long winter coat, not bothering to button it. From the glimpses she'd had out the windows, it was sunny and hopefully warmer.

James started to walk away, then turned and looked at her. "I'm being a grouch, aren't I?"

"Everyone has a bad day sometimes."

"Yeah, I certainly had one of those, but that's no excuse. I just have something on my mind."

"Oh?" She wanted to be a good friend and not pressure him to tell her, but this wasn't at all like James.

"It's no big secret," he said slowly, as though deciding whether he wanted to talk about it.

"If you don't want to—"

"No, I don't mind telling you. I've been invited to speak at a Wellness and Faith Conference in Wisconsin. Please don't say that's wonderful!" He sounded vehement.

"Isn't it?" she softly asked.

He rubbed the back of his neck and hesitated for a few moments before answering. "It's a great opportunity to talk about treating the whole patient, physically and spiritually."

"Yes." She watched his face, only now beginning to show light wrinkle lines. She hadn't thought about it before, but his temples were almost all gray.

"I don't think I can do it."

Her first thought was that he didn't want to leave Fern, but he quickly put that idea to rest.

"Fern wants me to go. Anabelle thinks I should. She even has me signed up to read in church so I can practice speaking in front of a group."

He sounded so miserable that she didn't know what to say. What was bothering him?

"I don't think I can do it. It's not that I don't want to." He was talking more to himself than her. He gave her a halfhearted grin, but his eyes were clouded with misery. "Thanks for not trying to encourage me. This is something I have to work out by myself."

He left the locker room without explaining. Candace was puzzled but also concerned. What could possibly cause James so much distress? He was one of the strongest people she knew.

She walked slowly to her car, still mystified. Was James dealing with some threat to his family or himself? Perhaps he'd been diagnosed with a serious illness. She knew it would rock his world if he couldn't take care of Fern.

Lost in thought, she was startled when James stepped out from the other side of her car.

"You gave me a scare!" she gasped. "I didn't expect anyone to pop out from behind my car."

"Sorry."

They looked at each other and laughed. The idea of being scared of James was more humorous than anything.

"I owe you an apology. I didn't mean to make a big mystery out of my problem. You're probably thinking I have a terminal disease or something."

That's exactly what she had been thinking.

"I'm fine," he was quick to say. "I'm the only one who thinks I have a real problem." He spoke rapidly as though he wanted to get it over with. "You see, when I was a kid, I had a bad stuttering problem."

"No one would ever guess that now."

"I know, but I've avoided public speaking because I'm afraid my stutter might come back in front of an audience. That's why I'm so torn about speaking at the conference."

"That's understandable. You're torn between wanting to share your wonderful ideas and being afraid of a physical disability returning. I don't know what I'd do in a situation like that."

She thought of the grief that never completely left her. It was affecting her ability to get on with her life, just as James was hindered by his fear of stuttering.

Much to her surprise, a genuine smile brightened his face.

"That's exactly it," he said. "Thank you, Candace. You don't know how much your understanding means to me."

She watched as he walked to his own vehicle and gave her a parting wave. Did it really mean that much to have one person understand exactly what he was going through?

Was there anyone who could really tap into her emotions and understand what it meant to lose a beloved husband?

She thought of Heath and also of people she'd met in her grief-counseling group. She'd moved beyond the need for regular one-on-one counseling, but she hadn't forgotten how much it meant to know she wasn't alone in her mourning.

Was this God's answer to grief? Could she heal by reaching out to others who'd lost focus in their lives, whether from the loss of a loved one or from other circumstances?

Turning, she walked back to the hospital. She was bone-weary, but there was one more thing she had to do before she went home.

Chapter Twelve

The curtain was drawn in Millie's hospital room, and none of the lights were on. Candace had to let her eyes adjust to the dim interior before she could see that both beds were occupied. The last time she'd visited, Millie was sitting up in an otherwise unoccupied room.

"Millie?" She whispered in case either of the patients was asleep.

"I'm here." The voice that answered her was weak.

Candace quietly moved up to the bed.

"I just thought I'd drop by to see how you're doing." She hadn't expected to find Millie flat on her back.

"They're never going to let me leave," she answered in a weary voice.

"Of course they are. As soon as your diabetes is—"

"They're going to put me in a home. No one says so, but I'm sure of it."

"That doesn't seem likely," Candace said, hoping she was right. Certainly Millie was too young to spend the rest of her life institutionalized. "Have you talked to your social worker?"

"She never tells me anything I want to know."

"Her hands are probably tied until you get an all clear from your doctor. You know, Millie, countless people live long, successful lives in spite of their diabetes. The secret is understanding how to manage it."

"How can I manage it living in my car—if I still have a car? I don't even know where it is. And I'll never be able to stick a needle in my stomach the way they want me to." She made a little noise that sounded like a muffled sob.

"Things have a way of working out." Candace knew how ineffective that sounded, and she'd said it several times before, but she was at her wit's end. Millie was seriously depressed, and she didn't have any answers to help her.

"It's getting a little warmer outside," she said, seizing on a neutral topic because her conscience wouldn't let her leave without visiting for a few minutes.

"Thank you again for the coat," Millie said. "It's hanging over there in that little closet. At least one thing I own is here."

"You'll get all your things back when you're ready to leave," Candace assured her, hoping that all the garbage bags full of her possessions hadn't been consigned to a Dumpster somewhere.

"Can you open the curtain for me?" an elderly voice asked from the other bed.

"Do you mind?" Candace asked Millie in a soft voice.

"No, it doesn't matter."

Candace opened the heavy drapery, letting the late afternoon sunshine flood the room. It relieved the feeling of oppression in the room, but Millie's only response was to turn on her side to face away from the light.

"Is there anything I can bring you next time I come?" she asked. "A magazine or something? Do you like to work crossword puzzles? Or maybe a little cross-stitch kit, something to keep your hands busy."

"No, nothing," Millie said in a weary voice. "Thank you anyway."

Candace did her best to sound cheerful when she said good-bye, but she was deeply frustrated. How could she help someone who didn't want to be helped? No, it wasn't true that Millie didn't want help. She was just too depressed to be receptive.

Candace took a deep look at herself. Had she rejected the comfort offered through grief counseling because she'd closed her mind to help the same way Millie had? She was trying to take small steps toward healing, but it was scary. She didn't want to give up any part of her love for Dean, but she knew he wouldn't want her to die inside because he was gone.

She hurried down to her car, badly needing to be with her family. Her eyes were moist as she thought of how little Millie had in her life. Was there no one out there who cared enough to visit the lonely patient?

The house was quiet when Candace got home, but before she could get her coat off, the silence was shattered by angry words and cries.

"Mother, wait until you see what Howie did!" Brooke said, storming up to Candace.

Her brother was crying, and his grandmother was trying to calm him without much success.

"I told her I'd buy another scrapbook," Janet said, blotting Howie's face with a tissue.

"He didn't have any right to ruin it!" Brooke insisted. "I'm the one helping Mom with the memory book."

"Please, tell me what this is all about," Candace said.

"I wanted to draw Daddy," Howie wailed.

"There's tons of paper in this house. You didn't have to scribble in the memory book!" Brooke shouted.

"I didn't scribble!"

Candace looked at her mother to enlighten her.

"Howie drew a very nice picture of his father on the first page of the memory scrapbook," Janet explained, sounding a bit frazzled.

"He didn't have any right to do that!" Brooke argued. "He messed it up."

"Did not!" Howie said, stamping his foot.

"Let me take off my coat, then you can show me," Candace said, not feeling at all up to refereeing a major dispute.

She didn't bother hanging up her coat, instead taking Howie's hand in hers and resting the other one on Brooke's shoulder as they paraded over to the table set up to work on the memory book.

"See!" Brooke said, pointing at the vivid drawing on the first page of the scrapbook. "He scribbled all over it with crayons."

"I drew a nice picture!" her brother insisted.

"No more arguing," Candace said in a stern voice. "Let me see what we have here."

Howie had used most of the first page to draw the figure of a man with yellow hair and a bright blue shirt. Certainly her son couldn't remember his father's light hair and blue eyes, but he'd managed to draw a recognizable image of Dean. Perhaps he went by the photograph in her bedroom, but one detail shocked her. In the picture, Dean was holding a stick that could only be Howie's attempt at drawing a golf club. Dean had been playing golf with friends when he collapsed and later died. How could a child who was not quite six recall such a telling detail?

Candace felt like she'd been kicked in the stomach. Her thoughts whirled around in her head, but Howie was eager to explain his picture.

"Daddy's trophy has a man with a stick like that," he said, pointing at the black object in his picture.

"Of course, he won the trophy in a city tournament, second place in his division." She thought how wonderful it was that Howie had this small reminder of his father's athletic ability. "It's a very nice picture, sweetheart."

"Mother, he shouldn't have colored in our memory book," Brooke reminded her. She had yet to uncross her arms.

"Wait, let's think about this," Candace said. "He was Howie's daddy too. Do you think the memory book would be complete without putting your brother in it?"

"No, but we can put in his baby picture or something. He doesn't even remember Daddy."

"I do too!" Howie vehemently disagreed. Candace could see the heat creeping up his neck.

"You were just a baby when he died. You only remember what Mom has told you."

Janet backed away from the group around the table, letting Candace know that this was her dilemma to solve.

"Daddy loved both of you so very much. Do you think Howie should help with the memory book?"

"He's too little."

"Am not!" Howie said indignantly.

"Think about this, Brooke," Candace said, drawing both of her children close by putting her arms around their shoulders. "You got to be with Daddy six years longer than Howie did. You have good memories in your head, like going to see the Fairy Castle in Chicago. Howie is too young to remember very much about his father. He needs the memory book even more than you and I do so he can know what a wonderful person he was."

Howie started to say something, but Candace gently laid her fingers over his mouth.

"How do you feel about that?" she asked her daughter.

"I didn't think about it that way. But, Mother, his picture's on the first page."

"How about this? I'll find a little photograph of Daddy. There's room to paste it on at the top of the page. Then you can use an ink pen to write his name and the title of the book. We'll use Howie's picture as a tribute to your father. I think he would be pleased that you let your brother be part of it."

Brooke stepped away from her mother's embrace, and for a moment Candace was afraid the battle wasn't over.

"I guess that's fair," Brooke said, letting her arms fall to her side. "But he has to promise not to draw anything else without your permission."

"Will you do that, Howie?" Candace asked, hoping his scowl didn't mean resistance.

"Yeah, I guess." He wiped his nose with the back of his hand.

"How about drawing more pictures on separate pieces of paper? Then we can decide which ones to paste into the book. That way you can draw a whole bunch if you want to, and you can help me decide which ones to use."

"Okay." His face brightened, and Candace hugged him against her with relief.

When she turned around, her mother was smiling at her.

"King Solomon couldn't have done any better," Janet said with a smile.

Candace wanted to fold up like an accordion and collapse on the spot, but her day with the children was only beginning. She hoped their teachers had gone easy on the homework, but Brooke shattered that hope.

"Mom, I don't get my math. You're going to have to help me, or I'll get a bad grade on my test tomorrow."

"I have to practice writing my *M*'s," Howie said. "My teacher said mine are too wobbly."

"Why don't you children get started while I make dinner," their grandmother suggested. "I thought we could have spaghetti."

Candace's shoulders drooped, and she glanced at her wristwatch, quickly calculating the hours until bedtime. Maybe tonight she'd go to bed right after the kids did. Without conscious intent, she said a little prayer for all the working single mothers who didn't have backup like her mom.

Anabelle cleared away the dinner dishes including Cameron's half-full bowl of homemade chicken noodle soup. The chicken stock and vegetables had simmered all day in the Crock-Pot, and her husband had added the frozen noodles at just the right time that afternoon. It was one of their favorite winter meals, and he must feel worse than he would admit to eat so little.

Before she could say anything about it, he sneezed loudly and reached for some tissues from the box beside his favorite chair. He was wearing his colorful red, yellow, and green wool robe in what he laughingly called his clan plaid. Cameron was proud of his Scottish heritage, and since he'd retired from his landscaping business, he'd spent a lot of time researching his background, tracing it back eleven generations.

"You sound miserable," Anabelle said. "Is there anything I can get for you, maybe some herbal tea?"

"Maybe later," he said, his voice hoarse and raspy. "I need to work on the reading schedule for church, maybe make a couple of phone calls. If my voice doesn't improve by Sunday, my whole schedule will be off."

"Don't forget to add James."

"Got it etched right here," he said, pointing to his full head of thick gray hair.

He sneezed again, and Anabelle could see that his nose was getting chapped.

"I'll set up the humidifier in our bedroom," Anabelle said, needing to do something to ease her husband's symptoms. "You should get to bed early. There's nothing like sleep to help you get over a cold."

"I think I'll turn in as soon as I walk Sarge."

The dog was enthusiastically chewing on a piece of rawhide in his corner of the kitchen, but one ear perked up when he heard his name. They'd adopted the ungainly pup from the county animal shelter on Christmas Eve when he was only ten weeks old. He was nearly double that age now, but his bloodlines were still uncertain. He was at least part German Shepherd, part mutt, and part pure energy. It had been love at first sight for Anabelle, but Cameron had been a bit reluctant to take on the training of a puppy. Now her husband doted on the dog, fully enjoying the companionship now that he spent so much time at home.

"You'll do no such thing," Anabelle said with mock severity. "You're much too sick to be traipsing around in the cold. I'll walk Sarge. It's not even dark yet, so I'll enjoy a nice long walk."

"I spent most of my working life outside," Cameron said, putting up a token fight. "A little fresh air won't hurt my cold."

"Maybe not, but curling up with a good book is a better idea."

Cameron grunted, his way of agreeing without actually saying so.

Anabelle hurried through the cleanup chores, then put on her winter jacket, knit hat, and mittens. That was all the signal Sarge needed. He pushed against her calves, waiting to be hooked up to his leash.

The afternoon had shown signs of moving toward spring; but this evening, the wind was blowing hard, pushing frigid air down the country road that wound its way past the Scotts' home. Anabelle walked on the blacktop, facing any traffic that might come her way. Sarge wasn't content to trot along at her pace. In spite of his rudimentary training, he still strained at the leash, intent on investigating the gravel and the withered stalks at the side of the road.

"Bad dog," Anabelle said when he gave a strong jerk on the leash and forced her to stop and guide him back beside her.

A sharp pain shot through her right hand and up her wrist, a return of the discomfort she'd experienced last week at the quilting session. She'd had a few pangs since then, but nothing like the fiery spasms that made her switch the leash to her left hand.

It felt awkward to have Sarge on her left, and he kept cutting across in front of her until she finally took the leash in her right hand again. Dusk was masking the roadway in a haze, and she took the failing light as an excuse to cut their walk short.

By the time she got inside the house, her hand ached all the way up to her elbow, and it didn't help that her fingers were stiff with cold.

There was a deep silence inside and out, the peaceful quiet that had appealed to them so much when they first bought their home on the outskirts of Deerford. Cameron often played music or turned on the TV, so she tried not to make any noise that would wake him if he'd nodded off. She needn't have bothered. Her husband came up behind her as she was gently massaging her throbbing hand.

"Hand bothering you again." It wasn't a question.

"Just a little. It'll be fine."

"You should see a doctor, get it x-rayed."

Cameron wasn't one to give orders. Even when their three children had been young, he made mild suggestions and told little stories to guide their behavior. Anabelle wasn't sure she liked being told what to do, even if he meant well.

"I'll see how it feels in a few days. I think some warm weather would do a lot for the ache."

Her husband started to say something, then paused for another big sneeze. "Maybe I will have that cup of tea, something to make me sleepy," he said.

"Why don't you settle down in bed, and I'll bring it to you."

He answered with another powerful sneeze, then headed toward their bedroom.

Anabelle boiled water and made two cups of herbal tea, putting them on a tray to carry to the bedroom. First, though, she wrapped her aching hand around one of the ceramic cups and let the warmth ease the pain. She wasn't going to tell Cameron how good the heat felt.

Tomorrow she was going to wear her old sheepskin-lined gloves to drive to work. There was no reason to see a doctor when a little common sense would take care of her problem. Anyway, warm, healing spring weather had to make an appearance pretty soon.

Chapter Thirteen

ELENA GATHERED HER DARK BROWN HAIR INTO A ponytail, the quickest way to style it for work. She checked her wristwatch for the third time in as many minutes, hoping she didn't have to leave before Cesar got home from his new job.

They'd both been surprised when he was hired on the spot at the monument company and told he could begin with the night shift right away. Apparently the college boy who had the job wanted to quit immediately.

Elena had sent her husband off to work with a thermos of hot coffee, a sack lunch, and a big hug, none of which did anything to improve his sour mood. He said he was thankful to get a job that would bring some income for the family, but she could tell the prospect of guarding tombstones instead of protecting people was hard for him to accept.

She looked in on her granddaughter, still sound asleep in her cozy bed, then left a note on the kitchen counter telling

Rafael to take the container of cookies when he dropped Isabel off at preschool. No doubt his daughter would remind him, but Elena wrote the note anyway. She knew that she tended to micromanage when she was nervous, but her son was good-natured about unneeded reminders.

It was only a short drive to the hospital, but a light snow had fallen during the night. She wanted to allow plenty of time in case the roads were slippery. One disadvantage of working the morning shift was that some days she had to leave before the road crews plowed and sanded the city streets.

She was zipping up her quilted nylon coat when she heard Cesar's car pull into the driveway. Late or not, she had to hear how his night had gone before she left for work.

One look at his face as he came through the door, stamping his boots and rubbing his hands together, told her all she wanted to know.

"Was it so terrible?" she asked.

"Terrible? No, it was just boring."

His cheeks were ruddy, and he hugged his arms across his chest without taking off his coat.

"Maybe you can take your old radio tonight, at least have something to listen to."

He shrugged and bent to unlace his heavy work boots.

"I have to go to work, but I left your breakfast in the oven, scrambled eggs and bran muffins," she said, still wanting to hear more about the job.

"Thanks."

"Have a good day, honey."

He only grunted. As a cop's wife, she was used to hearing little of what happened at his job. This time she suspected there wasn't anything to tell.

"Did you have trouble staying awake?" She hated to leave when he was obviously unhappy.

"I chewed through two packs of gum, but I managed."

She knew he'd only had a two-hour nap in the last twenty-four hours, so she let the subject drop. When he sat on a kitchen chair to pull off his boots, she gave him a quick hug.

"Things will look better when you've had a nice hot shower."

"Get to work," he said, not quite managing to make it sound like teasing.

Elena bent and kissed his cold cheek, then hurried out to her car.

All the way to the hospital she thought about Cesar's dilemma. He was miserable when he had nothing to do all day, but the guard job was a mindless chore compared to the responsibilities he'd had on the police force. She wanted to tell him to quit and look for something better, but his pride suffered when he couldn't provide for his family. He wouldn't give up a bad job just because he disliked it.

The hospital parking lot had been scraped free of snow, although it probably would have melted clean in a few hours. She didn't know the temperature, but the air felt milder than it had a few days ago.

She was walking toward the entrance when a voice called out to her. She stopped and looked back to see James trotting toward her, his coat flopping open and a gloved hand waving at her.

"Got time for a cup of coffee?" he asked.

Checking her watch, she was surprised to see that she was a few minutes early. She'd been so concerned about seeing Cesar before she left that it wasn't as late as she'd thought.

"My treat," James said as they both got steaming cups of the cafeteria brew to go. "Want a donut or something?"

"No thanks."

She hadn't had the chance to talk privately to James since their disagreement about the land donation, and she'd missed their easy camaraderie. They took the elevator up to the staff suite, taking cautious sips of the strong black coffee as they rode.

"So a drag-racing track, huh?" James started with a twinkle in his eye.

Elena laughed and shook her head, glad to know they were on the same side again. "I honestly don't think I could come up with a worse idea."

"And how's the family?"

"Cesar started a new job last night. Working security at the monument company."

James's eyebrows shot up. "I didn't know they needed a guard there."

"They had some vandalism last summer."

"How many policemen were laid off?" James asked.

"Half the department. Cesar just missed having enough seniority to be safe."

"Maybe Cesar will get called back before too long."

"Maybe." Elena didn't manage to sound upbeat.

The elevator door opened before James could respond.

"Anyway, a temporary job is better than none, isn't it?" he asked as they headed toward their lockers. "I started job hunting when the hospital had the big budget crunch last year, although I would have hated to make the boys change schools. It's good that Cesar has something to do."

"Not so good for him, I'm afraid." She didn't intend to disagree, but she'd brought her worries about her husband to work with her. "He's only been on the new job one night, but it sounded rather lonesome. There was nothing to keep his mind occupied."

James finished his coffee before taking off his coat. He seemed to be waiting for her to say something else.

"But Cesar would agree with you. Any job is better than none."

"If there's anything I can do—" he began.

"No, we'll be fine." Elena wanted to believe that.

James hung up his coat and said a halfhearted "have a good day" before hurrying off to begin his shift.

She felt even more heavyhearted as she watched her friend leave. When she thought about the anxiety James had with Fern, she was ashamed for stewing over her own problems so much. Everyone in her family was healthy, and she needed to be more optimistic for their sake. Plus spring was coming.

She took a few moments to pray that things would work out and to thank the Lord for all the good things in her life, for good friends like James and especially for the love of her family.

Anabelle enjoyed her job as nurse supervisor in Cardiac Care. She was more than comfortable with the demands of the job, and it was her greatest satisfaction to see heart patients return to normal lives because of procedures and care they received in the unit. She especially liked the education aspects: teaching patients to live a healthier lifestyle.

Some days, though, the efforts of the doctors and nurses weren't enough. They had lost a patient on the operating table that morning, a Deerford resident who worked at the post office. He'd struggled with heart problems for at least a dozen years, but he'd never come to terms with the need for a greatly altered lifestyle.

Anabelle took the loss personally, although there was no way she could've monitored his day-to-day living. Still, she regretted not being able to convince him to modify his diet, exercise regularly, and go to his doctor for regular checkups after his three earlier procedures at Hope Haven.

The whole staff was subdued, although it fell to the surgeon to speak to the patient's wife and two grown children. Of the staff, Anabelle was especially concerned about Charity, a recent nursing school graduate who'd only been assigned to the Cardiac Care Unit for a few months.

"But he wasn't even very old at all," Charity said for the third or fourth time.

"No, he wasn't," Anabelle agreed, recalling that the patient had been only sixty, more than two years younger than she was. "I know you're upset. If you like, you can take a little time off. I know it helps me to go to the chapel when something bad happens."

"You wouldn't mind?"

Anabelle saw tears swimming in the petite brunette's dark brown eyes and smiled sympathetically. "Take as much time as you need."

Anabelle felt in need of quiet time for prayer and contemplation herself, but her responsibilities as nurse supervisor kept her working through her lunch break. At least Charity returned in a calmer mood, able to smile and continue with her duties. Hope Haven Hospital was committed to treating the whole patient, but Anabelle knew that caregivers sometimes needed spiritual help too.

She thought of James and his commitment to faith-based nursing care. It really would be a shame if his long-past stuttering problem kept him from sharing his wonderful ideas at a professional conference. She wondered whether he'd made a decision about whether to go.

After the hectic morning, she felt drained of energy and badly in need of a snack. When she finally had a chance to take a short break, she hurried to her locker and retrieved her sack lunch and a bottle of water. Since his retirement, Cameron had gotten in the habit of fixing a sandwich or something for her every day, but he'd had such a restless night with his cold that she'd left without waking him.

The cheese sandwich she'd slapped together had all the appeal of a dish of dog food, and her banana was past its prime, but she settled down in the staff lounge to rest her feet and eat what she could. Unfortunately, the cap on her water bottle was on too tight. She struggled to twist it off without success.

She'd been too busy all morning to pay much attention to her hand, but it was throbbing again, making her wonder what the problem was. She put aside the second half of her sandwich and gently massaged her fingers and palm. Maybe on the way home she would stop at the drugstore and buy a topical pain reliever. She needed extra tissues and cold medicine for Cameron anyway.

Anabelle was too engrossed in her largely ineffective massaging to notice James until he walked up to her.

"Does that help your hand?" he asked, sitting down on the couch beside her.

"Not much," she admitted. "May be a touch of arthritis."

He raised one eyebrow, expressing his skepticism. "Is that your diagnosis?" he asked.

"I guess one reaches an age where little aches and pains are a part of life."

"In other words, you haven't seen a doctor," James said in his professional voice.

"You know how it goes," she said. "The pain will either get worse, and I'll have to have it looked at. Or it will go away by itself. I'm expecting the latter. Anyway, Cameron has a bad cold. I have to go to the drugstore and get home as soon as I can today. That reminds me, he may not be able to take his turn reading in church. That will throw the whole schedule off, and he'll be able to give you a turn sooner than he expected."

"Anabelle, I'm not so sure—"

"You'll never know whether you can do it unless you try."

"It doesn't work that way. It's not like putting on ice skates for the first time and venturing out on the ice. It's more like going on a roller coaster when you know you have motion sickness. The anticipation's bad, but actually doing it could be much worse."

"Are you talking about reading in church or speaking at the conference?" she asked sympathetically.

"Both—well, mostly the conference. I used to read to the boys when they were little. Maybe if I pretend that's what I'm doing in church, I can get through it. Maybe."

"There, you see. If your mind thinks you can do it, you shouldn't have any problem. You have a very pleasant voice,

James. Talk to a group the way you talk to a patient who needs you, and the words will flow. You'll forget you're talking to an audience and be able to concentrate on the message. I'm sure you can do this."

"If I had your confidence, I probably could," he said, still sounding doubtful.

"I bestow it on you, a gift from me." She held out both hands as though offering something tangible.

He laughed and shook his head. "It should be so easy."

"Either Cameron or I will call and tell you when you're reading and what the Bible verses are. You'll have time to practice ahead of time."

"Well, tell him I hope his cold gets better."

"Thanks, I will."

James got up and walked toward the door, reminding her that she'd overstayed her brief break. Then he stopped and looked back at her.

"Want me to open your water?" he asked.

"Please do."

He twisted it off with one easy movement and handed it to her.

"Have your hand x-rayed," he said as he left.

She had a childish urge to wrinkle her nose behind his back. When your best friends were nurses, you couldn't hiccup without getting advice.

"And aren't I fortunate to have friends who care?" she whispered.

Chapter Fourteen

CANDACE SAW AN UNUSUAL NUMBER OF STAFF members clustered around the second-floor nurses' station when she arrived for work Wednesday morning. It looked more like a social gathering than anything work related. Her first instinct was to ignore it and check in at the Birthing Unit, then she saw James standing on the fringe of the group. Anabelle was there too, and it wasn't like her to stand around visiting when it was time to start her shift.

She walked up to them and saw Elena in the midst of a rather heated conversation with another RN who worked the night shift in Cardiac Care. Elena was wearing pretty pink flowered scrubs that reminded Candace of a spring garden, but her friend's expression was anything but cheerful.

"Why should it matter what the land is used for, as long as the hospital gets enough money to make needed improvements?" Elena asked. She sounded a bit impatient, as though she'd already made the same argument several times.

Candace let her curiosity get the best of her and moved closer to the group. She shot a look at James, and he shook his head as though to warn her off. This only served to puzzle her more. She gave her full attention to the debate, if that was what it was, that was going on between Elena and several others.

"You read the newspaper editorial," Charity, a young nurse from Cardiac Care, said. "There's something not right about Leonard Baxter. He might be running for county land commissioner so he can help the developer get the hospital property."

"That was only implied," Anabelle said, offering her usual practical opinion. "We shouldn't take rumors as fact."

"The fact is," Charity said, "that no one wants a strip mall in Deerford. In the town where my grandparents live, an outsider came in and built one. It devastated the downtown area. Main Street is practically a ghost town."

"A strip mall is better than a drag-racing track," another nurse chimed in.

"I hate to think of stores boarded up in our town," a third nurse said.

"You don't know that would happen," Elena countered, obviously upset. "We should be concerned about updating the hospital. What will happen to Hope Haven if we can't keep up with current technology?"

"Maybe we should wait until the hospital board comes up with other options before we make up our minds," James said in a quiet voice, perhaps trying to defuse the situation.

Candace hated to see Elena on the losing side of an argument, but she wasn't at all sure that the property should be sold to a developer. Most of the businesspeople in Deerford were longtime residents who had a personal stake in the welfare of the community. The hospital could always use the money, but any decision should benefit the whole town.

"There certainly are things that could be done to update the hospital's technology," Candace said. "But we have to trust the hospital board to make the best decision."

"They don't work with patients the way we do," Elena argued. "With them, it's numbers and statistics."

"At any rate, it's not our decision," James said in a reasonable voice that only seemed to irritate Elena.

"It *is* our responsibility to speak up," she insisted. "The staff's in the best position to know what the hospital needs to improve the level of care."

"As far as I can tell, you're the only one who wants to sell off the land to the first buyer who comes along," Charity said.

Candace was surprised by the young nurse's aggressive stance, but she didn't think anyone there had enough facts to decide what should be done with the legacy. She agreed with James: It was a decision only the hospital board could make.

"Time to get to work," Riley said, giving Charity a stern look.

The group slowly dispersed, but James went up to Elena and said a few words to her. Candace couldn't hear what he said, but knowing James, he was probably trying to calm her. Elena could be as coolheaded as any nurse on the staff when it came to medical emergencies in the Intensive Care Unit, so her emphatic stance on the land issue was a little puzzling.

Candace had to admit, though, that something about Leonard Baxter puzzled her. He was campaigning hard and obviously spending serious money in an effort to win a minor county position. She didn't even know what a land commissioner did, but she was pretty sure it wasn't a full-time position.

Time to get moving, she told herself. She looked in on a tired but smiling mother who had given birth during the night, and that was her last calm moment for several hours. Wendy, a young woman who looked like she should still be in high school, checked into the Birthing Unit with her even younger-looking husband. Candace had her hands full reassuring the nervous father-to-be and preparing the mother-to-be for what was to come. Again, she sadly noted, the girl hadn't attended any childbirth classes.

If there was one cause she could embrace wholeheartedly, it was a countywide campaign to promote childbirth classes. Hope Haven had an excellent program—which she taught—but too many pregnant women slipped between the cracks. She knew the local obstetricians promoted the classes and took turns teaching, but many of their patients came from small towns without hospitals. Wendy's doctor was a general practitioner with hospital privileges, but he rarely had patients in the Birthing Unit. Candace could only hope that this would be an uncomplicated birth. Staff doctors were always available to step in; but sometimes, outside physicians were reluctant to call for help.

She sighed in anticipation of a long day.

By the time the shift ended, Wendy still hadn't delivered. A C-section was a strong possibility, and Candace hoped there would be good news when she came to work tomorrow.

She hurried to Millie's room, only intending to look in on her for a few minutes. The room was sunny and bright, a nice change from her last visit, but Millie wasn't there.

"They wheeled her away," the elderly woman in the second bed informed Candace.

"In a chair?" Candace had a vision of Millie strapped to a gurney.

"Yeah, a wheelchair. You can wait, if you like. Maybe she'll be back soon."

Candace knew a plea for companionship when she heard one, so she spent a few minutes visiting with the roommate. It soon became obvious, though, that it might be a long time before Millie returned. Candace cut short the visit in the kindest way she could, promising to return another time.

When she got home, there was a vehicle parked in her driveway, a dark blue midsize SUV that was vaguely familiar, although she couldn't place it.

As soon as she stepped inside the house, Howie rushed out to enlighten her.

"Auntie Marion's here!" he cried out, racing back to the living room as soon as he'd delivered his news.

Candace smiled broadly and slipped out of her coat, then hurried to greet one of her favorite people.

Marion Crenshaw was Dean's unmarried aunt and one of the strongest people Candace knew in spite of her rail-thin frame and advancing age. Her spiritual strength and counsel had helped immensely during Dean's funeral, and they couldn't have had a more welcome visitor.

Marion was wearing a lavender pantsuit with a deep purple turtleneck sweater and a big smile. When she stood to embrace

Candace, she looked frail enough to be blown over by a strong wind.

"Aunt Marion, it's so good to see you! How long can you stay? Brooke will be happy to give you her room. What a nice surprise!"

She glanced at her mother, who gave a slight shrug, indicating that the visit was a complete surprise to her too.

"Oh dear, I'm afraid it's just a pop-in. I'm not in Deerford alone actually. Two of the ladies from church are with me. We're on our way to a conference on missions, but driving from Des Moines to Chicago in one day is a bit too much for me. I couldn't be so close to you and the kids and not say hi."

"We have room for them too," Candace said, quickly deciding to give them her bed and to skip her small group therapy.

"No, no, we're all checked into a motel. I can't believe how pretty Brooke is. She has her father's light coloring and beautiful blue eyes. And such golden hair. And Howie, you must have grown a foot since I last saw you." She ruffled his coppery brown hair, and he grinned with delight.

"You'll at least stay for dinner," Candace urged. "I'll go get your friends at the motel. I'm sure Mom can work her magic and fix something nice for all of you."

"Thank you so much, but none of us is much for a big meal in the evening. We had a big lunch just a couple of hours ago, so I think we'll all go to bed early. I'd like to drive into Chicago before rush hour in the morning. We figure we can do that if we get up around four."

Candace was as disappointed as her children when Marion declined, but mostly she was terrified to think of Dean's beloved aunt negotiating the freeways into the big city. The trucks were frightening enough, but Des Moines traffic couldn't prepare the seventy-five-year-old woman for the way Chicagoans darted from lane to lane at breakneck speeds.

"Are you sure you want to do that?" Janet asked. "You could take a commuter train from the outskirts of the city to wherever you want to go."

"That's a good idea. I'll talk it over with the other ladies," Marion said.

"Come see the picture I drew," Howie said, taking Marion's thin hand in his.

"Have the children shown you what we're making to honor Dean?" Candace asked.

"It's a memory book," Brooke said. "Howie wasn't supposed to draw on it, but Mom said we should leave his picture on the front page."

"What a wonderful picture of your father," Marion said, lifting the scrapbook to see it better. "He was a good artist, too. Now that I think of it, I have a picture he drew for me when he wasn't any bigger than you. I may still have it. I used to put little mementos in a tramp-art box my grandmother gave me."

"What's tramp art?" Howie asked.

"During the Great Depression when people didn't have much, some artists would cut up cigar boxes—they were made of wood then—and make beautiful things. The more I think of it, the more I'm sure that's where I put your father's pictures and other little things that mean a lot to me. Would you like to have his drawing for your memory book?" She asked Howie but looked at Candace for approval.

"That would be wonderful," Candace said, "if you're sure you want to part with it."

"I wouldn't so much be parting with it as adding it to a memorial for my dear nephew. Whenever I come to visit, you can get it out for me to see again."

"Thank you, Auntie Marion!" Howie said enthusiastically.

"That would be nice," Brooke said. "Thank you."

She didn't say that it would be much nicer to have a drawing by her father than by her brother, for which Candace silently thanked her.

"In fact," Marion said, picking up the scrapbook to admire Howie's picture, "I probably have some other odds and ends you might want to include. Photographs, certainly, but I've always been a saver. No telling what I'll find if I look. I've been thinking that it's time for me to do some serious cleaning."

"I can't tell you how much we'd appreciate anything of Dean's that you want to share," Candace said, gently hugging the older woman.

"Now," her mother said, "I've got a peanut butter pie in the freezer I've been saving for a special occasion. It won't take any time at all to thaw it in the microwave. Let me put the teakettle on, and we'll have a special treat in honor of your visit."

"Peanut butter," Marion said as she sat down on the wing-backed chair and took in the children with her gaze. "Your daddy did love it. I used to make a double batch of peanut butter cookies whenever he came to visit. I do believe he never left without eating every last one."

Howie sat at her feet, and after a minute's hesitation, Brooke joined him. They loved hearing stories about their father, and Aunt Marion had tales to tell that they'd never heard before. Candace thought about helping her mother with the dessert, but she wanted to hear stories about Dean as much as her children did.

When Janet was ready for them, Marion insisted on sitting around the kitchen table. Candace could see that she was fatigued after driving all the way from Iowa, but she was as reluctant as the children to have her visit end.

The children were spellbound as their great-aunt told them about the day their father was born.

"In those days, no one knew whether it would be a boy or a girl, but your grandpa was so certain he'd have a son that he bought him a toy truck. I think I have a baby picture with that very truck."

Candace let her mind wander to the Mississippi River that had inspired the memory book. Every major waterway had tributaries, smaller streams and rivers that fed into the main flow. She thought of Aunt Marion as one of the wonderful tributaries on the river of Dean's life. The more she thought about it, the more important it seemed to include all the wonderful people who had contributed to his journey through life: his extended family. This book was a way for the children to understand who their father was. It should include everyone who was important to him.

Before Marion left, she thanked her again for her contribution to the memory book, briefly telling her how Millie and the river had inspired it. Marion's eyes were moist when they parted, and Candace had to hold back her own tears.

Chapter Fifteen

By the time Candace came to work Thursday morning, Wendy had given birth to a healthy baby boy. He was a tiny little creature weighing an ounce under six pounds, but his lungs were in fine form. He squalled and wiggled with so much gusto that he managed to work one tiny arm free of his little shirt.

No matter how long she worked at this job, Candace didn't think she'd ever lose the sense of wonder she felt with every newborn. But mothers were her primary responsibility, and Wendy was so exhausted she'd hardly touched her breakfast.

The new mother had elected to breast-feed her baby, but the initial attempt didn't go well. Baby Jacob screamed and resisted. Wendy held him as though she was afraid he'd break, and her stiff arms didn't comfort him.

When he returned to his portable crib and was wheeled away to the nursery, she broke down in tears.

"I can't do this," she sobbed as Candace tried to comfort her.

"It's not unusual for first-time mothers to get off to a slow start nursing. You had a long labor. You're exhausted. Things will improve when you've rested."

Candace said all the comforting things she could think of. Her patient mopped her damp face with tissues and accepted a water with a straw from Candace.

Wendy had looked young in the labor room with her blonde ponytail and apple cheeks. Now she seemed more child than adult, and Candace couldn't help worrying about her distress. Taking care of a baby was no small undertaking, and as far as she knew, only the young husband had come to the hospital to be with her.

"You have a wonderful adventure ahead of you," Candace said in her most soothing voice. "Your baby will grow into a sturdy toddler, and you'll love him more with each passing day."

Candace was afraid the advice she'd given the young mother wouldn't be enough, but help had to come from somewhere. She was going to recommend a parenting class, but it was too soon to suggest it. Meanwhile, she'd tell the other staff members to give Wendy as much help as possible with the routine of taking care of a newborn.

She remembered how nervous she'd been on the day Brooke came home from the hospital. But she'd been greatly blessed with a caring husband willing to do his share and more, not to mention her mother's and sister's help. And her mother-in-law, Dorothy, had come to stay for several weeks, giving Candace time to recover and get used to caring for a new baby. Her daughter's early days went smoothly, thanks to the love and care of a virtual army of helpers. She hated to think how difficult things could have been without them.

In fact, it was because of Dorothy that she had a calling plan that allowed her unlimited long distance. She frequently phoned her mother-in-law and father-in-law Don. Dean had been their only child, and they'd both been devastated by his death. They were in an assisted-living facility in Florida and were still able to get out and enjoy the warm, sunny weather. But neither would ever recover from the loss of their son. Dorothy, especially, was frail, although she didn't like to talk about her cardiac problems. Don, like his son, was a kind, generous man who did everything he could to make his wife's life more endurable, hiding his own pain as much as he could.

Candace left her phone with Wendy overnight so she could make long-distance calls, but tomorrow she wanted to call her in-laws. Aunt Marion had been so excited about the idea of a memory book that she thought maybe Dean's mother and father would find some comfort participating in the making of it.

Before she left for home, she looked in on Millie and left her some magazines. Perhaps she'd find an inspirational article that would give her some insight into her situation. Candace had the uncomfortable feeling that she should be able to counsel the diabetic woman herself, but she was too conflicted in her own faith to find the right words.

On the way home, she thought about Dean's family and the river of life. When she first started the memory book, she'd thought of all the places that had meant something to the two of them, but she'd been shortsighted. People mattered the most, not locations or events. The flow of memories began with the people who were important to him, and that meant all of his family.

Aunt Marion was his father's only living relative, but Dorothy came from a large, close family. She had three sisters, two still living, and Dean had been blessed with a multitude of cousins, including his boyhood companion, Luke Spillers. Some had come to his funeral, but a few had scattered to far places like Australia and Hawaii. Dean had always wanted to travel and visit his relatives, but it wasn't to be. Still, they should all have a place in the memory book.

She made up her mind to contact as many as she could by phone or letter. As soon as she got her cell phone back, she'd call Dorothy for names and addresses.

After dinner, Brooke was eager to do more on the scrapbook.

"I don't have a single bit of homework," she proclaimed.

"Me neither," Howie said, getting a scornful look from his sister.

"You never do. You're in kindergarten."

"Mommy, I do too!"

"Yes, you do," Candace quickly said, "but let's not quarrel. I have a good idea for the memory book. I'm going to try to contact all of Daddy's relatives. I think he'd like to have his whole family in his book. He does have quite a few cousins, you know."

"Does that mean they're my cousins too?" Brooke asked.

"Second cousins, I think," Candace said.

"Does that mean we can't do anything on the memory book until you talk to all of them?" Brooke sounded less than pleased.

"Not at all. We'll have plenty of room at the back of the book for photographs or other things they might want to contribute."

She looked over at the crowded card table, already overflowing with photographs and pictures Howie had drawn.

"I have an idea. We really don't have enough room on that table. I thought we could move the whole project down to the rec room. We could spread out on that old Ping-Pong table that was here when we moved in."

"It doesn't even have a net," Howie said.

He didn't like the lower level, even though the main room had light wood paneling, blue patterned carpeting and fluorescent lights to make it a cheerful place to hang out.

"We don't need one to use it for the memory book," Candace explained. "I thought we could scrub the table and lay everything out in the order it should go. That way we can plan ahead instead of just pasting randomly. Think of Daddy's life as a big, broad river. We want to start at the beginning when it's just a little stream."

"We have his baby pictures," Brooke said, immediately grasping the idea. "Howie's and my first pictures will come somewhere in the middle."

"That's it! And if the Ping-Pong table gets crowded, we can use the card table too."

"Do I have to draw my pictures down there?" Howie asked.

"Of course not, sweetheart. We'll just put things on the table so we can see how much we have."

"Maybe we'll need two scrapbooks," Brooke suggested.

"That's a possibility. Now, who will help me clean the table?"

"I will." Brooke went to get cloths from her grandmother's ragbag.

"How about you?" Candace asked her son.

"If you're going down there, I guess I'll go too," Howie grudgingly agreed.

Howie's reluctance to go downstairs was a problem for another day, but maybe working on the memory book there would help him forget his fears. She could remember not liking her grandparents' cellar with its shelves of dusty jars of preserves and the dark place behind the furnace. In fact, her sister Susan, older by three years, had once teased her by pretending to lock her down there.

"Come on, you two! Let's do this!"

Cameron shuffled into the living room in his slippers and robe carrying a box of tissues with him. He had dark circles under his bright blue eyes, and his usually neat gray hair went every which way from napping most of the day. He didn't often get sick, but when he got a head cold, it was a whopper.

"Are you sure you don't want me to stay home this evening?" Anabelle asked. "It's not our regular meeting, just an extra session to work on all the new cloth we've been given."

"No, you run along. I'm not very good company tonight. I'll just walk the dog and watch some TV. There's a program on the History Channel that I want to see."

"You can't walk Sarge in your pajamas," his wife said. "And there's no reason to get dressed just for that. I have time before I pick up Genna. It's my turn to drive."

"Well, if you're sure . . ." He sounded more than a little bit relieved.

Anabelle put on her coat and got the leash, eager for a brisk walk. It wasn't as cold as it had been, and the roads were clear of snow. Her gangly pup frolicked around her legs until she hooked him up and started out the door, remembering at the last moment to pull on her thick woolen mittens.

Her right hand still ached, a dull throb that she could ignore when she wasn't using it, but holding Sarge in check sent spasms of pain through her fingers. She switched hands when they reached the road, but the dog bounded to her left and yanked the leash out of her grasp.

"Bad dog," she whispered under her breath, but she blamed herself for not keeping a better grip. Sarge was always so excited to be outside that hanging onto him was a challenge. She was trying to teach him good doggy manners, but it was slow going. Now she had to tease him back to her so she could grab his leash.

Sarge had other ideas. He raced across the road and into a field while she trailed after him with no real hope of catching up.

"Sarge, here boy, good dog, here Sarge."

He was only doing what dogs loved to do: sniffing, exploring, and running. She knew he'd return to her when he'd had his fun, but she needed him to come now.

"Sarge, here Sarge." She tried to keep her voice neutral, knowing that her pet wouldn't return to her just to be scolded.

He looked up as if to say "Come play with me," then put more distance between them.

She stooped down, holding her hand out to him. Unfortunately, she didn't have a treat with her to entice him closer, but she didn't want to go back to the house and leave him running loose. They didn't have a lot of traffic on their road, but all it would take was one car driving too fast to hit the dog.

"Here Sarge, good doggie, here Sarge."

She finally stood upright when her knees began to protest, but Sarge was only a dark streak against the withered stalks in the field. There were still patches of snow where drifts had yet to melt, and all she would accomplish by trying to chase him would be wet slacks and soggy running shoes.

She stood and watched as best she could in the twilight. When she did corral him, he'd probably have filthy feet and a coat full of burrs. She couldn't leave Cameron with the tedious job of picking them out and giving him a bath in the laundry tub downstairs, not when her husband was still miserable from his cold.

Resigned to waiting until the dog decided to come to her, she wished she had her cell phone. She needed to tell Genna to go ahead without her. Maybe with luck, she could get there for the second half of the work session.

Sarge teased her by coming close, but not close enough for her to grab him. His little doggy brain must have known he was being naughty, because he made a game of almost letting her catch him.

"Rascal," she said under her breath, watching intently for a chance to capture him.

Finally her patience paid off. He came close enough for her to step on the end of his leash, restraining him long enough for her to grab his collar. She gripped tightly until she could secure the end of the leash in her hand. This walk was over.

As she'd feared, his coat was peppered with dried burrs. After a quick call to Genna, she sat down on the kitchen floor with Sarge and a pair of scissors, cutting out the stubborn burrs when she could and picking at others.

"He got away from me," she said when Cameron came into the kitchen to see what she was doing.

"Want me to do that?" he offered a bit halfheartedly.

"No, I've got most of them. I'll just run him through the tub to get the mud off. You go watch your program."

"You sure?"

He looked at her with watery eyes, and she didn't have the heart to involve him in the dog's bath.

If there were ever times when she doubted her sanity for adopting a puppy, it was during Sarge's baths. She kept his leash around her wrist while she filled the laundry tub with water, not wanting to chase him around the basement, then put on a big plastic apron. It was always a toss-up who got the wettest while she scrubbed and rinsed him. She lifted him into the tub and got on with it, wondering how much heavier he was going to get.

Twenty minutes later she led him upstairs and hurried to change into dry clothes, trying to ignore the increased pain in her hand.

The group was busy when she got to the quilting session, two of the members at work on portable sewing machines they'd brought with them.

"You look pink-cheeked," her friend Genna said when they were seated side by side at the worktable.

"Sarge led me on a merry chase," she said, going into details without making any move to begin work. She rubbed her aching hand under the table, but Genna was too sharp-eyed to miss the gesture.

"Your hand is still bothering you, isn't it?"

"A little. I had to pick out burrs and give the dog a bath before I could come. He's getting to be a handful."

"How long has your hand been bothering you?" Genna sounded more like a doctor than a doctor's wife.

"Awhile. But I don't think it's anything serious." It couldn't be anything serious. She didn't even want to consider the possibility of giving up her beloved quilting. Her breath caught in her throat when she thought of holding her newborn grandbaby in several weeks.

"Anabelle, you really must see a doctor and get it x-rayed."

She massaged her sore hand for a moment, then managed a smile for her well-meaning friend.

"You're right. I'll see about getting an appointment tomorrow."

Chapter Sixteen

"COMPASSION." JAMES ROLLED THE WORD OVER HIS tongue, loving the sound and the meaning behind it.

During his years of service as a nurse and as a medic in the Gulf War, he'd worked with many medical professionals. He'd known some who had great knowledge and expertise but lacked compassion. Others, no better trained, seemingly worked miracles because they cared deeply about their patients.

After prayerful consideration, he accepted that this was a message he had to share with others. As a dedicated Christian, it was both his obligation and his privilege. For that reason, he'd signed the agreement to speak at the Wisconsin conference. Even now, as he began work on Friday morning, his acceptance letter was in the mailbox at home, the flag up, waiting for the mail carrier to pick it up.

He didn't regret his decision, but the weight of it was a heavy burden. He was going to give it his all, but it remained to be seen whether his stuttering would return to thwart him.

Fern was proud of him and pleased that he was going to share his ideas at the conference. Her support meant a lot, but he was also thankful for friends on the staff at Hope Haven. He planned to pick their brains for examples to use in his presentation. He thought, for example, of the way Candace kept visiting Millie, hoping to learn something about her background that would help her move forward. As things were now, it was very likely that the patient would have to move to a county home. James hated to see her warehoused that way when she was still capable of earning a living and being a part of the community.

He sighed, satisfied with his decision but still apprehensive.

"You sound like you have big worries," Elena said, coming up behind him at the nurses' station.

"Nothing that serious," he said with a short chuckle. "Just thinking about the presentation I'll be making at the Wellness and Faith Conference. I thought I'd talk about nurses who wear designer scrubs to make patients feel better," he teased.

She placed her hands on her hips and turned side to side. "I just thought I'd wear something springlike because the weather can be so drab this time of year." She picked a bit of loose thread off the sleeve of her bright pink top patterned with little white violets.

"I get tired of choosing between hospital green and surgery blue."

"Blue goes very nicely with your eyes," Elena said with a smile.

Anabelle hated to be an alarmist. Now that she'd made an appointment with a doctor at the Deerford Orthopedic Center, she didn't think her hand hurt enough to take up his time. She flexed it as she doled out medications in little plastic cups. No pain. Or at least not enough to send her running to Deerford Medical Services across the street from the hospital. But since she'd made the appointment, she supposed she should keep it.

Or maybe, she could ask James to take a look at it. His experience as a medic didn't make him a doctor, but he had a huge store of common sense and practical knowledge. If he told her that she needed to see an orthopedic specialist, she wouldn't feel that she was going for nothing. Maybe he could recommend a simple solution, a brace or something. The more she thought about it, the better her idea seemed. She hoped he would take his break at the same time she did.

Luck was with her. She went to the cafeteria around eleven thirty and spotted James at a table against the wall. She hurriedly selected a bowl of beef noodle soup with crackers and went to his table.

He wasn't alone, but she was happy to see that the inhalation therapist at his table was nearly through with her meal. She didn't want to ask James for medical advice until he was alone.

"Mrs. Scott," the plumpish, black-haired younger woman said, "James just told me about his invitation to speak at a conference. Don't you think he'll do a wonderful job?"

"He certainly will," Anabelle said, raising her eyebrows in a questioning glance at James.

"I mailed my acceptance today," he said with resignation.

"Well, I have to run," the inhalation therapist said. "Good luck writing your speech."

As she gathered up her tray and left, Anabelle smiled broadly at James.

"Congratulations," she said. "I know you'll do a marvelous job."

James pursed his lips and looked at her without commenting.

It was immediately obvious that James didn't want to talk about reading at church or going to Wisconsin. They had a short conversation about their families and then Anabelle casually mentioned the problem with her hand.

"It really doesn't seem bad enough to see a doctor," she said. "What do you think?"

"Make a tight fist," James said.

She did, trying not to react to the twinge of pain.

"Now stretch your fingers as much as you can."

It was uncomfortable, but not excruciating.

"What do you think?" she asked.

James grinned. "I think you're trying to get me to tell you that you don't need to see a doctor."

"Well?"

"Anabelle," he said, nodding his head, "you need to get it checked out."

"It might get better by itself."

"Sure, if you don't use it for a week or so. Or it might not get better."

Anabelle knew she'd been busted.

Elena wandered down to the cafeteria when the time came for her lunch break, but she didn't have much of an appetite. She brought a book with her to enjoy over a cup of tea and sat down at a table for two at the far end of the room. She'd just settled down when she was surprised to see Cesar come into the big room and look around.

She waved to get his attention, and he ambled over.

"I thought you'd be sleeping," she said.

"Too much on my mind to settle down," he said a bit sheepishly. "I'll get a good nap before my shift. I brought you some lunch. Good thing, if that tea is all you're having."

"I'm not very hungry," she admitted.

"You will be when you see this," he said, removing the contents of a brown paper bag. "My specialty: club sandwich with ham and provolone cheese and tortilla chips. And look what I found at that little shop you like so much, your favorite."

He put a square glass jar on the table and invited her to read the label.

"Red pepper and artichoke tapenade," she read, touched even though she wasn't sure they could afford fancy foods.

Cesar had yet to get his first paycheck, and neither of them knew how much it would be.

"You know I can't possibly eat all this."

"I knew you'd say that, so I brought extra napkins. We can share."

Elena found she did have an appetite, mostly because it was so good to see her husband in a cheerful mood.

"Cesar, good to see you." James loomed over their table, a smile of pleasure on his face.

"Hey, same here." Cesar stood and shook hands, inviting James to get a chair and join them.

"Maybe for a minute or two. I'm just about due back on the floor." He grabbed an unused chair from another table and straddled it.

"I hear you have another job," James said.

"Temporary job," Cesar said dismissively. "Have some chips. They're great with tapenade."

"I've had my lunch, thanks. Well, maybe one, just to taste it."

He helped himself to a chip from the bag and dipped it into the peppery concoction.

Elena's attention was on her half of the sandwich as the two men talked about a favorite sport, basketball.

"I'm helping with middle school intramurals," Cesar said.

"You're what?" Elena asked.

"Seventh and eighth grade basketball. One of the fathers dropped out, so I'll be helping until the season is over."

"When will you sleep?" Elena frowned, always concerned that her husband get his rest.

"That's great," James said before Cesar could answer. "I didn't know you were into coaching."

"My boyhood dream," Cesar said with a soft laugh. "I wanted to coach the Bulls, but hey, this is fun, too. I'll have a blast with middle school players. They're about the same age as the boys in Rafael's Scout troop when I was the leader."

"We'll have to trade Scouting stories sometime," James said. With that, he left, and Elena fretted as her husband talked about his plans for the day. She didn't have the heart to rain on his parade, but when was the man going to get his rest?

Elena appreciated her husband's surprise lunch, but her mood was gloomy as she went back to Intensive Care. He needed something to keep him occupied during the day, but she was afraid he was taking on too much, forgetting the long night of tedious security work ahead of him. Worse, he'd volunteered to work the weekend because the company hadn't found someone to cover Saturday and Sunday nights. His pay still wouldn't be anywhere near his police salary, but he said that he needed to make up as much of the shortfall as he could.

She would have to think of some way to keep Isabel quiet and happy after church. Cesar would be exhausted by the end of the week, but he wouldn't neglect his granddaughter if she wanted attention. More importantly, she needed to look into extra hours for herself. She didn't want her husband to carry the whole burden.

And what was this about coaching kids' basketball? When the season was over, would he want to do baseball too?

She sighed, suspecting that her big, manly husband had a little boy inside wanting to get out. Maybe all men did.

Anabelle liked when she was very busy, rushing to do all that she could for patients and balancing the doctor's instructions with her own commonsense practices. Today wasn't one of those days. In fact, the afternoon was unusually quiet with no new cardiac patients admitted all day. She should take it as a good thing—maybe everyone was finally following doctor's orders.

She paused for a moment at the nurses' station where she monitored all the activity in the unit. With nothing urgent to do for the moment, she looked at her hands, laying them flat on the desk. When had the network of blue veins become so prominent? When had the slight wrinkling begun? They were steady when she held them out, but the flesh over her palms seemed to be stretched tighter than it once had been. Her hands were getting old, and she hadn't really noticed until the right one developed a minor ache.

Even though she wasn't exactly apprehensive about her appointment with the orthopedic doctor, she couldn't help worrying about his diagnosis. How could she continue in her job if her hand needed surgery? Worse, what about the grandbaby?

She was thankful to the Lord for her many blessings, foremost of which were her three children. Her son Evan was a fine young man, and Kirstie had overcome the tragedy of losing her leg in a bicycle accident at age ten. She'd matured greatly in recent years, gently but firmly letting her overly protective mother know that she could stand on her own now.

Anabelle smiled inwardly, knowing that her other daughter, Ainslee, had fought the same battle after she announced that she was having a baby. But anticipating the arrival of a new life was bringing great joy to both of them.

She rubbed her hands together, thinking of the time when she could hold her first grandchild in her arms. The aches and pains of aging were nothing compared to this prospect. Her whole day brightened when she remembered that she was meeting Ainslee for coffee after her shift. Cameron had discouraged her from coming to the house because he didn't want her to get his cold, so they were meeting at Diner on the Corner across from the hospital.

"Mrs. Scott, a patient insists on speaking to you," a young RN said as she rushed toward the nurses' station. "It's

Mr. Brown. He's refusing his medication. Says it makes him nauseated."

"I'll talk to him," Anabelle said, automatically rushing toward the uncooperative patient.

Maybe he had a real problem, and maybe he only wanted attention. Either way, it was her job to treat each and every patient with love and compassion.

Ainslee was waiting for her at a small table near the rear of the restaurant when Anabelle got there. Her daughter looked radiant, her face glowing with happiness at over seven months along. Her dark mahogany red hair was swept back from her face giving her a regal look, even in a pale green sweatshirt and jeans.

"Mother, how was your day?"

Anabelle motioned for her to stay put when she tried to stand up to greet her. "Fine, but more importantly, how did your doctor's appointment go?"

"Everything looks great. He mentioned not to gain too much weight from now on, but I guess that's a reasonable expectation."

Anabelle ordered tea, and Ainslee insisted that she get a muffin too.

"You know you're always starving after your shift," she said.

"Are you taking all of your vitamins?"

Ainslee gave Anabelle a disapproving look. "You're only allowed three questions."

"Vitamins?"

"Check."

"How are your birthing classes going?"

"Smoothly."

"Have you found out the gender yet?"

"No."

"How are you—"

"That was three, Mother."

Anabelle sighed. "Very well."

"How's Pop doing with his cold?"

"You know how miserable being sick makes him, but he'll get over it soon."

"Well, give him my love," her daughter said. "He's going to make the world's most wonderful grandpa."

"And—" Anabelle said.

"And you'll make the world's most wonderful grandma."

Anabelle nodded her approval.

"In fact, the baby will be doubly blessed on both sides of the family." She rubbed her stomach.

They chatted until Ainslee had to leave to meet her husband, and Anabelle felt refreshed and uplifted after their visit. She got all the way home before she remembered the pain in her hand. Maybe she was right. Maybe it was something that would go away without medical attention, although she really couldn't take the chance.

Nothing would stop her from holding her precious grandchild.

Chapter Seventeen

Candace had already heard the bad news. Millie would definitely be going to the county home as soon as there was an opening. There was no way to know whether that would be in a day, a week, or months. Meanwhile, the hospital staff had done all they could for her diabetes, but her doctor was still concerned about circulation problems.

When Candace peeked into her room after work on Friday, Millie was alone, sitting in a chair and staring out the window at a sky filled with dark clouds.

"You're looking well today," Candace said by way of greeting.

It was true. Millie's salt-and-pepper hair was done up in a neat bun instead of hanging lankly on either side of her narrow face. Slightly pink cheeks had replaced the gray cast of her complexion, and she was wearing a pretty print housecoat instead of a hospital robe, a gift from one of her nurses.

Millie didn't acknowledge the compliment, instead speaking immediately about her greatest concern.

"I'll be going to the county home," she said in a morose voice. "They'll have room as soon as someone dies."

"There are other reasons for vacancies," Candace was quick to point out. "They take all ages, not just the elderly. Sometimes a relative steps in to offer a home, or one of the younger ones gets into a rehab program. Some people only stay a short time. That may be what will happen to you."

Her homeless friend looked at her with eyes dulled by despair.

"You know I lost my husband," Candace said in an effort to take Millie's mind off her problems. "My children and I are making a memory book, a scrapbook of mementos that will help them remember him. I owe you a big thanks for giving me an idea for the theme."

"Me? What did I do?" She sat up a little straighter in the wooden-armed hospital chair.

"Your story about going down the Mississippi with your grandfather made me think of life as a river, people and events flowing together. It was so nice of you to share that memory with me."

"It was the happiest time of my life," Millie said in a muted voice.

"Your grandfather sounds like a wonderful person," Candace said. "Everyone should have someone like him. I feel the same way about my husband." Candace smiled to herself then continued. "In order to fill the memory book, I've contacted my husband's relatives. Some I've never even met, but they were all eager to contribute something, a picture, a shared experience, a newspaper clipping—whatever they thought would add to the story of his life."

"That's nice," Millie said, showing a glimmer of interest.

"Sometimes we lose touch with extended family. It takes a tragedy to remind people of their bond. Perhaps there's someone in your family who would like to hear from you. Maybe a cousin or an aunt or even a second cousin."

"No, there's no one who wants to hear from me."

"Are you sure? One of my husband's cousins lives in Australia. Can you imagine, they were practically inseparable when they were young, but they hadn't seen each other in ages."

"Sometimes relatives don't see each other because they don't want to."

"Oh, Millie, there must be someone you'd like to see again. Wouldn't your brother want to know how you're doing?"

Millie stared off into space without answering.

"Well, I have to get home," Candace said, discouraged by the woman's lack of response.

"Thanks for coming," Millie said in a halfhearted voice that seemed to mean the opposite of what she said.

Maybe she should forget about Millie and stop trying to interfere in her life, but Candace had a stubborn streak when it came to helping others. She wasn't quite ready to give up.

"You know, Millie, none of us is ever completely alone. If you like, I can ask the hospital chaplain, Pastor Tom, to come speak to you."

Millie looked directly at her, something she hadn't done since Candace came into the room. For an instant, there was something different in her expression, a glimmer of light in her eyes, then it faded and she turned her face away.

"No thanks," she said in a flat voice that discouraged Candace from saying more.

After the visit she hurried down to her car, unable to forget the sudden glimmer of hope on Millie's face. Was there anything else she could have said or done to fan the flames of faith? Had she turned so far from God that she'd lost her ability to bring His comfort to others?

She could only think of one more thing she could do for Millie. All the way home she prayed for her.

Anabelle had taken her turn at working on a Sunday. She'd hated to miss church, but at least Cameron felt a lot better and went without her. The one good thing about working on a weekend was that she had Monday free for a morning appointment at the orthopedic center. Her hand hardly hurt anymore, but Cameron and James had convinced her to see the doctor.

Dr. Kramer was a short, rotund man with a warm smile that endeared him to his patients. Cameron had seen him for a back problem before he sold his landscaping business, and they both had a lot of confidence in him.

"It feels so much better this morning that I feel silly taking up your time," she confessed in the small examining room.

"Nurses," he tut-tutted. "Worst patients in the world except for doctors. We'll get an X-ray and see what we have here."

The technician who worked with the orthopedic doctors positioned her hand on a piece of foam that allowed him to get X-rays from several different angles. After a short wait, she saw Dr. Kramer again.

"Have you been doing anything unusual with your hand lately?" he asked.

"I quilt a lot, but I've been doing that for some time."

"No, I don't think sewing is the cause."

He frowned, and she wanted to ask him what was wrong. But years of working with doctors had given her the patience to let him tell her in his own way.

"You haven't lifted or pulled anything especially heavy?"

"No, not that I can think of."

"The hand is the most abused part of the body. When it's overused, the tendons swell and cause pain and irritation. You have hand tendonitis."

"What can I do about it?"

"I'll give you a prescription for an anti-inflammatory medication. Ice compresses are helpful too. Use your hands as little as possible. If the pain doesn't ease up, you might try wearing a hand brace. Come back if you still experience pain in a week or two."

"I was afraid I might need surgery."

"Only as a last resort. I don't think it will come to that."

She left the doctor's office feeling relieved. The X-ray hadn't shown any sign of arthritis, a diagnosis that could have impacted her ability to do her job. She felt optimistic about getting better without extreme measures.

One thing was sure: She wanted two fully functional hands when her first grandchild made his or her debut into the world. She thanked the Lord that her problem was minor and prayed as she did every day that Ainslee would have a safe delivery and that her child would be healthy.

Cameron was in the kitchen when she got home. He'd filled a small plastic bag with ice cubes and was attempting to crush them with one of his smaller hammers.

"What are you trying to do?"

"Make myself a little ice pack." He gave the bag of ice another whack and studied the results.

"We have an ice pack in the freezer. What you have there is going to leak. Why do you need it?"

He rolled up the sleeve of his red and blue plaid shirt and extended his right hand. Anabelle immediately saw the swelling on his index finger.

"Sprained my finger," he said in a disgruntled voice. "I thought a small bag of ice would work better than the big ice pack."

She took his hand in hers and looked at the injured digit.

"Sure looks like it," she agreed. "How did you do it?"

"I wouldn't say that I did it. Sarge's idea of a morning walk is a little different than mine."

"The dog did that?"

"I wanted to close the garage door before we got started—don't want the neighbor's cat having another litter in there. I had the leash wrapped around my hand so the dog wouldn't get loose on me again. He gave a hard yank, and there you have it." He held up his swollen finger again and watched while she double-bagged the ice and wrapped it in a dishtowel.

"Sarge did that just by pulling on his leash," she mused, handing the pack to her husband.

"He's a strong little guy," Cameron said without rancor.

"You may have just solved a mystery. Dr. Kramer wanted to know whether I've lifted or pulled anything especially heavy lately."

"So what did he have to say about your hand?"

"He said it was tendonitis and to come back if it doesn't improve, but I don't think that will be necessary now that I know the primary cause."

"Sarge?"

"Sarge." She nodded assent. "He pulls when I walk him."

"So the cure may be not walking the dog?"

"I don't see how we can do that. He has too much pent-up energy if he doesn't get out."

"No, that's not an option," Cameron said, attempting to wrap the baggie of ice around his finger.

"It's time he learns some manners," Anabelle said in a determined voice.

"Obedience school," Cameron said as if reading her mind. "Too bad we slacked off after Diana helped us get started. I blame myself for not doing a better job as his trainer."

"It's not your fault. Sarge is rather high-spirited. We're not lion tamers, so I guess we'd better get some professional help."

"I'll look into it right away," her husband said. "Meanwhile, I'll do the dog walking. I don't want you to injure your hand any more than you have."

"Do you want to see a doctor about your finger?" she asked.

"No, I'll be okay. I'll just keep ice on it."

Her husband ambled into the living room to occupy his favorite chair and settle in for the evening.

James held the piece of paper that Cameron had given him between his finger and thumb as though it might ignite at any moment. He had a date to read in church, and Anabelle's husband had made sure he had the Bible passage well ahead of time. James brought it to work with him, along with his own copy of the Bible, intending to read through it during his lunch break. He wanted to be so familiar with the verses that they were etched on his memory. Hopefully, that way he would be less apt to stutter.

When he'd first looked at his assigned reading, I Corinthians, chapter thirteen, it had seemed impossibly long. Could he possibly get through all thirteen verses without stumbling over the words?

Just as he'd planned, he used his short break to go over and over it in the staff lounge, quickly eating his sack lunch so he could fully concentrate on the words.

One thing gave him hope. It was a passage about love, one that he especially liked. He could already recite parts of it without looking at the book, and reading it over increased his confidence.

"If I speak in the tongues of men and of angels, but have not love, I am only a resounding gong or a clanging cymbal."

He frowned at the text as he read "clanging cymbal." It was a potential tongue twister, and he'd have to practice it a lot to be sure it didn't trip him up. It was in verse one, so it would be terrible if he started the reading with a stammer.

"Love is patient, love is kind. It does not envy, it does not boast, it is not proud."

He silently mouthed the passage. As a lover of words and a man of faith, he responded to the great wisdom behind the verse, trying to absorb the full impact of the lesson.

How often had he heard sermons that concluded with the thirteenth verse?

"And now these three remain: faith, hope, and love. But the greatest of these is love."

"James, are you talking to yourself?"

He was startled to see Elena standing in front of him with a puzzled expression.

"I guess I was," he said sheepishly. "Actually I'm going through the chapter I'll be reading in church. Anabelle thought it would be good to read before a group before I have to speak at the Wisconsin conference. I haven't had much practice in public speaking."

"You can't practice mumbling to yourself," she said with a teasing smile. "You have to do it in front of people."

He nodded in agreement, but he didn't think Fern and the boys were enough of an audience to help him overcome his trepidation.

"What are you reading?" Elena asked.

He told her, and she smiled at the familiar verses.

"I like that choice," she said, "but you need to read it to others, not just to yourself."

He shrugged, suspecting that his friend had something in mind, probably something he wasn't going to like.

"Tell you what," Elena said, "I'll ask Penny Risser if we can use the chapel for a short time after our shift ends. I think she's the one who would have to give permission. Just leave it to me. I'll see that you have an audience. In fact, I think it would be nice if some of the staff got together for a Bible reading and silent prayer."

He knew it was a great idea, but was he up to it? Wouldn't it be even harder to read to his co-workers than to the congregation at church?

"Consider it done."

He hadn't seen Elena with such a happy smile since Cesar was laid off, so for that reason alone, he supposed he should go along with her idea. It was worth a little extra anxiety on his part to see her energetic self again.

"Okay," he agreed. "And how is Cesar doing at the monument company?"

"Bored to tears, I guess. We haven't had much together time lately. By the time I get home from work, he's off coaching. I worry that he isn't getting enough sleep, but at least it makes him happy to be doing something positive. It's sad how many of the boys don't get enough time with their fathers. Cesar is really good with kids."

"Has he ever thought of changing careers so he could work with young people full-time? I've heard most police officers retire fairly young and do something else for a while," he said, the glimmer of an idea coming to him. "Has Cesar ever thought of taking some college courses to prepare him for a second career, maybe as a teacher or coach?"

"He's really never had the time."

"Basketball season is nearly over. Maybe he could start picking up a few courses online." Now that James thought of it, he was sure Cesar would be great working with kids full-time.

"That might be something he would love. It would give him something to look forward to in the future. You know more about computers and such than I do. I bet Cesar would like to bounce some ideas around with you. I'm absolutely sure that he doesn't want to work security after he retires from the force. He's been so much happier since he started helping with boys' basketball."

"I'd be glad to talk to him about the possibilities. I had a friend who finished medical school when he was in his mid-forties. People wondered why he bothered at his age, but now he runs a clinic in one of the poorest countries in the world, saving countless lives. It's never too late to try something new."

"I want to see Cesar happy, no matter what he wants to do. I think I'll mention your idea the first chance I have."

"Well, back to work," James said. "Thanks for your idea of reading in the chapel."

"What are friends for?"

Chapter Eighteen

"MOM, I NEED MORE TISSUES!"

Brooke's voice carried down to the kitchen where Candace was fixing hot lemonade for her sick daughter. Brooke couldn't be feeling more miserable, which was a terrible way for her to spend her twelfth birthday. Candace took the cup of steaming liquid out of the microwave and put it on the tray with cinnamon toast sticks she'd just fixed for her. A quick visual check showed that she had everything: a cold pill in a plastic cup, a napkin, and a teaspoon in case Brooke wanted to sip her beverage that way.

"Be right up," Candace called out.

Brooke had hardly touched her dinner last night, and this morning she'd been running enough of a fever for Candace to suggest she stay in bed. It had been a long time since Candace had taken a personal day off work to take care of one of her children. Her daughter had insisted that she could stay home alone and would be well enough to still have her birthday dinner with several friends, but Candace had overruled her. She spent the morning trying to contact parents to let them know dinner was canceled. She didn't like missing her Monday shift, but her mother was going to be busy with an emergency dental appointment and Candace couldn't leave Brooke home alone.

When she carried the tray into the room, Brooke was propped up on pillows, her pink flowered quilt pulled up under her chin. Her eyes were watery, and her nose was beginning to match the pink of her coverlet. She wasn't often sick, but when she got a head cold, it was bad. It was a sure sign that she felt really awful because she wasn't even reading or listening to her MP3 player.

"All gone," she said, holding up the tissue box.

Candace arranged the tray on her daughter's lap, cautioning her that the lemonade was hot.

She went to the bathroom cupboard where they kept a supply of paper goods, but there wasn't a new box of tissues. Candace had followed her mother's system her whole life: When you use the last of something, write it on the grocery list, and she was sure tissues hadn't been on the list when she'd done the Saturday shopping. A roll of toilet paper would have to do.

"Mom!"

Candace entered Brooke's room and handed her the roll. Brooke tore off a piece and blotted her swollen eyes.

"I want the bell."

"Oh dear, I have no idea where it is."

When Brooke was in first grade, she'd had the chicken pox and had to stay in her room to keep from infecting Howie. Candace had given her a little bell to ring when she needed something, and she could still hear that bell ringing. And ringing. And ringing.

"Could you look for it? Please, Mommy." Brooke asked so sweetly that her mother didn't have the heart to refuse. Especially on her birthday.

"My head hurts," her daughter said, running her hands through her matted hair, another sign that she was feeling poorly. One of the first things she usually did in the morning was brush her curly blonde hair.

"Why don't you close your eyes and rest? Give the cold pill time to clear your head."

"How can I do that when I have to blow my nose every thirty seconds?"

"Give it a try," Candace said sympathetically. "I'll go look for the bell."

As Candace started down the short flight of steps, the empty tissue box in hand, the phone rang. Sometimes it felt as if she spent most of her time at home going up and down stairs, and she worried that it was hard on her mother. *Still, one problem at a time*, she thought, dashing to answer the phone.

"Hello," she said a bit breathlessly, catching it on the fifth ring.

"Hello, this is Lorraine Denton, the nurse at Howie's school."

"Is something wrong?" Candace asked with a feeling of dread.

"I don't think it's anything serious, but Howie didn't feel well in class. He has a slight temperature, and I think you should come get him. I'll keep him in my office until you get here."

"Of course, I'll be there as quickly as I can."

She hurried upstairs to her daughter's room.

"Honey, your brother got sick at school. I have to go get him. You'll be all right home alone for a little while, won't you?"

"Mother!" Brooke looked at her with watery eyes. "I'm old enough to stay home by myself."

"Of course you are. I'll be right back."

Several minutes later, she was pulling into the parking lot at Rishell Elementary School. She picked up her pace as she headed toward the entrance. The day was chilly but it wasn't the biting cold of the past few weeks. Candace pulled open the school doors and made a beeline for the office.

Howie came to the office with the nurse, wearing his coat. He looked pale and wan, and Candace wanted to hug him but didn't. Her son was beyond appreciating public displays of affection.

"Thank you for coming so quickly," Mrs. Denton said. "I'm due at the middle school in a few minutes. School nurses are spread a little thin in the district."

"Thank you for taking care of him," Candace said.

Howie gave a little tug on her coat, just enough to indicate he was ready to go.

"Did you want to get his assignments from his teacher?" the office secretary asked.

"No, I won't bother her now," Candace said. "I'll wait and see how long Howie will be out."

They left together, and she settled him in the backseat. When they got home, she helped Howie out of the car. She spent the rest of the afternoon between Brooke's and Howie's rooms trying to comfort two kids who felt miserable. At one point, she presented Brooke with a cupcake, and Howie dragged himself out of bed to help his mother sing "Happy Birthday," and he hardly had enough energy to make it back. By the time her mother came home with a temporary cap on her tooth, Candace felt as though she'd been put through a wringer.

When both children had finally drifted off, Candace wandered down to the lower level of the house where the mementos of Dean's life were waiting to be assembled in the memory book.

She circled the table, picking up photographs, touching the sports letter he'd won in high school, trying to bring him to her through the objects that reflected his life.

Was it going to help her children remember their father? Howie had been too young to know him. Brooke's memories would fade as she grew into adulthood. Certainly they would cherish the book and its contents, but what did it mean to her? She'd come far with the patient and loving help of Lila, Megan Gallagher, and the rest of her support group, but would she ever have a normal, happy life without Dean?

What did the completion of the memory book mean to her? Could pictures on a page do anything to fill the empty spot in her heart? She remembered Olive's testimony about the book she'd made for her husband and felt a glimmer of hope.

"My darling," she whispered softly. "You wouldn't believe what an awful day I've had, but I'd gladly have all my days be just as hard if you were still beside me."

She didn't realize she was crying until a warm tear slid down her cheek.

Chapter Nineteen

ELENA RUBBED HER TEMPLES, THANKFUL THAT HER shift was over for the day. It was only Tuesday, and already she was looking forward to the weekend break.

Her weariness was her own fault, of course, for volunteering to work Saturday and Sunday. She rarely worked a seven-day week anymore, but she was worried about finances. Cesar's job as a security guard paid next to nothing compared to his police salary, and she wished he could quit it. They had almost no time together now that he was working all night.

Izzy would be home by the time she got there, and seeing her would be the bright spot in her day. Cesar would be off doing his basketball coaching, the one activity in his life that he enjoyed right now. Maybe James's idea had been good. Even if Cesar was called back to his police job, someday he would be eligible to retire. It would be wonderful if he could step into something he really liked instead of taking the kind of menial jobs many retired cops had to do. His pension would be good, but there was no end to their expenses.

Elena allowed herself a weary smile at the thought of extending her own career until she was seventy or eighty, not that it was a possibility. She'd be forty-eight this year, which was more than well on the way to fifty. She hadn't given it much thought until Cesar was laid off and she realized how crucial her salary was to their well-being.

She was on her way down in the elevator to keep her promise to James. He was tremendously popular with the staff. It wouldn't be any trouble getting a group together in the chapel so he could practice reading in front of people.

The hospital's lovely little chapel was open to visitors and staff at all times, but she probably should ask Penny Risser for permission before rounding up friends to listen to James. The CEO's executive assistant was in charge of scheduling just about every event in the hospital, and she could be touchy if she wasn't consulted.

Reluctantly she headed toward the hospital director's office on the first floor, hoping Penny wouldn't give her a hard time. Sometimes it seemed that the woman existed to disapprove of things. Elena said a silent prayer for patience on her part and hoped that the executive assistant was in a good mood.

The outer office was a jungle of plants, thanks to Penny's love of every growing thing. She had a legendary green thumb. Once, the story went, she cut off a branch from a dead lilac bush to tie up another plant. With sunshine, water, and Penny's special touch, the dead branch had bloomed with fragrant purple lilacs.

The outer office was empty, and the door to the inner sanctum was closed. Elena checked her watch, deciding to wait a few minutes. Penny had a well-deserved reputation for being difficult, but her office certainly showed a more sensitive side. Her desk was surrounded by lovely plants, some in big containers and others hanging from the ceiling in colorful ceramic pots. An especially large tub held a rubber plant that was more tree than houseplant. She walked over to it, wondering when it would be too huge to stay in the office. Elena loved a garden but certainly didn't have Penny's green thumb. Cesar teased that she had the touch that withered, although that wasn't entirely fair. She did well with spider plants. Hers kept having baby plants, and she always had extra to give to friends.

It seemed that Penny wasn't going to be back anytime soon. Lovely as the plants were, they didn't hold Elena's attention today. She had far too much to do to linger any longer. She was just leaving when the outer door opened and two men entered. They nodded at her and started to tell her that they had an appointment with Mr. Varner, but she quickly explained that she'd only been waiting for the executive assistant. She quickly left, but not before her curiosity had been piqued.

Leonard Baxter had been easy to recognize with his lantern jaw and lacquered salt-and-pepper hair. The other man was a stranger in an exquisitely tailored navy suit and a shirt so white it seemed to shimmer. The latter was carrying a huge portfolio.

"Is there something I can help you with?" Penny asked, nearly colliding with Elena as she headed down the corridor.

Penny's green and red plaid jacket dazzled the eye, but it was her razor-sharp voice that got Elena's full attention.

"I just..." It took her a moment to remember why she'd come there.

"Just what?"

"The chapel. I want to get permission to use it."

"Anyone can use it. You don't need permission." The executive assistant eyed her skeptically.

"Yes, I know, but this is different. I want to gather a group of staff to listen to one of us read from the Scriptures." She didn't want to betray James's stuttering problem, but her reason for asking seemed lame.

"I still don't see why you're asking me, unless you had some other reason to come here."

"No, it was only a courtesy," Elena said, throwing back her shoulders so she looked even taller than her five foot eight inches. "You are in charge of scheduling events."

She should have known Penny wouldn't be intimidated by her stern tone or her extra inches.

"Go ahead and do as you like so long as you don't prevent patients or visitors from coming into the chapel."

"Of course not."

The office door opened, and her heart skipped a beat. The hospital's chief executive officer had a commanding presence most of the time, but today his tie was crooked and his face was unusually flushed. Elena badly wanted to ask him why the two men were there, but it was out of the question, and certainly none of her business.

"Penny, I wondered where you were. I need you if you're through here." He absentmindedly nodded at Elena. "Is there something we can do for you, Mrs. Rodriguez?"

"She just wanted permission to have a group use the chapel for a Scripture reading."

Penny was so used to being the go-between for her boss that she automatically answered. For once Elena silently thanked her for being so overbearing.

"Anyone connected to the hospital can use it," Varner said, his dismissive tone letting both of them know that such trivial matters didn't merit his attention.

"I told her that," Risser said in a self-satisfied voice.

"Well, thank you. I just wanted to be sure we wouldn't be interfering with anyone else."

"When were you planning this?" Penny said in a strident voice as Elena started to back away. "I'll put it on my calendar to cover all our bases."

"In two days."

"Thursday then, I assume after the first shift is over."

"Yes." She hoped James didn't have some activity with his boys then. She would hate to come back and ask Penny to change her calendar.

"That's settled then," the CEO said, still looking at her with a searching expression, holding the door so Penny could go back into the office.

Elena got all the way to her car, her coat unbuttoned and her gloves still stuffed in her pocket, before she began to wonder whether Varner was involved in some plot to sell the hospital's land. *Plot*—there was a word she'd never used before, and she laughed out loud at her suspicions. The hospital administrator had every right to consider selling the hospital property. He was a good Christian with a reputation for fairness and sound judgment. It would be totally out of character for him to be involved in anything that wasn't strictly aboveboard, but that didn't mean he couldn't be taken in by Baxter and the man with him.

Would Cesar be home yet? She doubted it. The intramural basketball games usually kept him busy until nearly dinnertime. She thought of going to see him, but a gym full of noisy boys tossing a ball around wasn't conducive to having a serious talk. She drove home, trying to decide what to say to him when she had the chance. It would be like him to say she was putting the cart before the horse, but she couldn't help feeling uneasy about the fate of the hospital property.

When she got home, Rafael was sitting cross-legged on the living room floor playing a board game with Izzy. Elena watched them for a minute before Izzy noticed her, letting the love she felt for her only child and his daughter soothe her nerves. Their heads were close together, Isabel's hair as black as her father's, and Elena said a silent prayer, thanking the Lord that her son was such a good father. Of course, he'd had his own father as an example, and she was doubly thankful for that.

"*Buela*," Isabel said, using her pet name for her grandmother, "I'm winning!"

"She's really a tiger at this game."

"I'm not a tiger, Daddy," Isabel said giggling. "It's your turn."

"It looks like you're having fun," Elena said, smiling down at both of them.

"Mom, can you believe this girl is beating me for the third time? Oh, Dad called. He'll be home a little late because he wants to get a haircut on the way."

Elena badly wanted to talk to Cesar, but she had to content herself with starting dinner.

As it happened, her first chance to be alone with her husband came after Isabel was tucked into bed and Rafael had left to go over some music with one of his band members. By then it was nearly time for Cesar to go to work.

"We've got to stop meeting like this," he said, playfully kissing her forehead as he looked for the heavy boots he needed to keep warm on his outside patrols.

"There's something I must tell you."

"Well, we only have about five minutes before I have to leave." He carried his boots to a kitchen chair and started to pull them on over heavy woolen socks.

"I'm afraid something fishy is going on at the hospital."

As quickly as she could, Elena told him about the two men she'd seen at the hospital administrator's office.

"You could be imagining things," Cesar said thoughtfully. "You don't have any evidence that they're up to something that might not benefit the hospital."

"Isn't it enough to be a concerned employee?"

"Afraid not," he said, his brow creased with concern. "It could backfire if you try to get involved."

"Stop being a cop for just one minute," she said, disappointed that her husband didn't see how serious the problem was.

"Last I looked, I wasn't a cop anymore."

"You will be again," she said, sorry that she'd touched a sensitive subject. "Do you think I should just do nothing?"

"For now, but I still have connections. Let me see what I can find out about this Baxter. If he's up to something, you can be pretty sure he's been involved in other shady things. For now, though, I have to get to work."

"I wish you were liking it more there."

"If I don't get called back to the department soon, I'll start looking for something else," he said. "Meanwhile, I don't want you working any more seven-day weeks. We can get along fine without that."

"I am tired," she admitted, "but you're the one who isn't getting enough sleep."

"Basketball season is nearly over for the kids, but meanwhile, it makes my day to help out with intramurals. Gives me something to look forward to."

"I know."

Elena kissed his cheek and watched as he pulled on his heavy coat and thick suede gloves. At least the days were getting warmer, although the temperature still dipped uncomfortably low at night.

"Miss you," Cesar said, giving her a quick hug before he went out the door.

"Miss you too," she said, but her husband wasn't there to hear.

Chapter Twenty

By Wednesday evening, both of her children were feeling considerably better, but Candace didn't think they were well enough to go back to school the next day. Janet was more than willing to take care of them until they were completely healthy, but Candace felt a little guilty putting so much on her mother. Still, she had little choice. They were shorthanded in the Birthing Unit, and babies had a habit of being born at their own convenience, not their nurses'.

At least Brooke had abandoned her bed and any notion of replacing the missing bell. Howie had been content to play quietly in his room, rather a relief since she hoped they didn't exchange illnesses. His tummy was still touchy, and her daughter insisted she couldn't go back to school as long as her nose was red. All she needed was for Howie to pick up Brooke's cold, and Brooke to come down with Howie's stomach virus.

Howie went to bed early without protesting, a sure sign that he wasn't 100 percent yet, but Brooke was restless now that she felt better.

"Can we work on the memory book, Mom?" she asked after her brother had settled down for the night.

"That's a good idea. Grandmother Crenshaw sent so many pictures and things by overnight mail that we need to lay them out in the order we want to use them."

"I had another idea," Brooke said in a hesitant voice, as though expecting her mother to object.

"Oh?"

"I found Daddy's Bible in the bookcase downstairs. He must have read it a lot because he highlighted a lot of parts. He even wrote notes on the pages."

"He taught adult Bible class for a while," Candace said, recalling a memory of Dean, pencil tucked behind his ear, rifling through his stack of books as a basketball game played on the TV in the background. "He especially loved the book of Luke. He said it took him back to the time when Jesus was teaching and preaching and made him seem even more alive."

"So the highlighted verses were ones he especially liked?" Brooke asked.

"Yes, I suppose so."

"I thought maybe we could put some of them in the memory book."

"That sounds like a good idea," Candace said, a bit surprised by her daughter's suggestion.

"I've figured out how to do it. I'll write them out on separate pieces of paper, then glue them in. That way, if I make a mistake copying one, it won't be on the scrapbook page. I can use the pretty art paper I got for Christmas, and we can get out all of your special stamps."

"I can see you've really thought this out. It's a lovely idea."

"Is it okay if I take Daddy's Bible to my room later to work on it?"

"Of course. I'm sure it would please him very much to know that you want to do this for him."

For the next hour, the two of them worked hard to put pictures in chronological order, spreading them out on the old Ping-Pong table ready to be pasted into the book.

"We'll never get all this in," Brooke said, looking down the rows of mementos. "It's going to be hard to decide what to leave out. Do we really have to put in all of Howie's drawings?"

"I've been thinking about that. Some of the pictures Grandma Crenshaw sent are duplicates of ones we already have. I wonder if you and Howie would like to make memory books of your own. I'm sure we have enough to fill two smaller scrapbooks."

"Mom, you're a genius! Howie can put all his pictures in his book, and I can have my own special book."

"Some of his drawings will go into the big book too," Candace warned. This project was taking on a life of its own, and she couldn't be happier for her children's sake. Brooke started going through the piles, sorting out duplicates to be divided between Howie and her.

Long after everyone else was asleep, Candace lay awake thinking of the memory book. It was bringing her family even closer together and reminding them that Dean was still very much with them in spirit.

What should she make of Brooke's idea to use his favorite Bible verses? It was almost as if Dean were guiding her, wanting his beloved daughter to know how much the Lord's Word had meant to him.

Then it hit her. Brooke wasn't blaming God for taking her father away. If anything, her faith was strengthened as she worked to preserve his memory. Her daughter was reading Dean's Bible because she wanted to know what was important to him. In their innocence, neither child was questioning why he'd been taken from them.

Candace twisted and turned in the big bed that still seemed so empty without her husband beside her. She tried to pray, but her thoughts came out in fragments, spilling all over like a pyramid of children's alphabet blocks. The harder she tried, the more inarticulate she felt. She found it difficult to reconcile the image of a loving Lord with the God who had taken her beloved Dean from her. Deep in her heart, though, she knew Dean believed all things happened for a reason. He would want her to turn to God for comfort and strength, and she vowed to try harder.

She didn't know what time it was when she finally fell asleep, but she awoke Thursday morning feeling as though she'd hardly slept at all.

The house was still quiet, and she tried to get ready for work without waking anyone. The children were going to stay home another day, and her mother would need all the rest she could get to keep up with them.

Rather than make noise getting breakfast, she decided to have something in the hospital cafeteria. She was on her way downstairs when a soft voice called out to her.

"Mommy?"

At first she thought it was Howie, but Brooke called out again, and there was no mistaking her voice. Candace quietly peeked into her room.

"Are you okay, sweetheart? Need anything before I go to work?"

"I just wanted to thank you."

"Thank me for what?"

"It was a wonderful idea to make a memory book for Daddy. I dreamed that he was watching me paste in pictures. He was really happy."

"That's such a nice dream," Candace said, glad to know Brooke had such a pleasant dream instead of one of her nightmares.

She bent over and kissed her daughter's forehead, a gesture Brooke would have found too babyish most of the time.

"Go back to sleep and have more good dreams," Candace said, pulling the quilt over her daughter's shoulders.

She wished she could follow her own advice and crawl back into bed, but even as she stood outside her daughter's room, some new soul might be struggling to enter the world. The prospect of holding new life in her arms was enough to send her hurrying off to work.

The cafeteria wasn't crowded when she got there, but a few staff members were taking advantage of the reasonably priced breakfast. Candace went through the line and selected orange juice, cereal, and coffee, not a hearty breakfast but enough to keep her going until her lunch break. She didn't look around to see whether there was anyone she knew, preferring to be alone with her thoughts.

She still didn't know exactly how she felt about Brooke's interest in her father's Bible. Was it just one more way for her daughter to try to connect with her lost parent? Or was her daughter developing a deeper faith, one that would help her deal with the loss of her father?

Was she failing her children by not doing more to foster their faith? She went to church and took them to Sunday school, but was she truly living her faith? Since Dean's death, she felt numb. Would she ever be able to recapture the feelings of rapture that she'd experienced in earlier days?

What would Dean say if he could speak to her again? It meant so much to him that their marriage was a shared spiritual experience. She wasn't turning away from God, but she needed help reconciling her strained faith to move beyond her grief.

"You look like you're a world away," a familiar voice said.

She looked up to see James standing beside her table with a tray of scrambled eggs, hash browns, toast, and coffee.

"At least you're not going to overeat," he teased. "Mind if I join you?"

"Not at all."

She nodded at the empty chair across from her, surprised by how glad she was to have him share the table. He was certainly better company than her tortured thoughts.

"So how are you doing?" James asked in such a compassionate voice that she knew he wasn't asking about her health.

"Oh, I'm getting by." She drank the last of her orange juice, appreciating her friend's concern but not ready to talk about the prevailing loneliness in her life. "We have a family project, making a memory book about Dean. My mother-in-law helped out a lot by sending us a big packet of pictures and things. I know she'd like to see the finished book. Maybe I can take it with us the next time we visit, although that won't be anytime soon."

She was talking to divert James from asking more questions about her grief. He'd been supportive when she went to counseling and was always willing to listen, but she'd reached a point where the only one who could help her lived inside her skin.

"There's an easy solution to that," he said, spearing the eggs on his fork. "Take pictures of the memory book pages and send them to her."

"I'm afraid my photography isn't up to it."

"I can do it for you. I enjoy playing with my digital camera. It would be a new challenge to record the pages of your book. As soon as it's done, let me know—if you don't mind my seeing it, that is. You can send your in-laws a photographic copy of it."

"That's awfully nice of you, James, but I wouldn't want to put you to that much trouble."

"As I said, if it's too personal—"

"No, not at all."

"Think it over," he said with a pleasant smile. "I'm more than willing to do it."

"I will, thanks. By the way, I have 'orders' from Elena to stop by the chapel on the way home this afternoon. She said something about your reading."

"I'm just going to practice the verses I'm reading in church Sunday. I haven't done much public speaking..." His voice trailed off, and he gulped the last of his coffee.

"It sounds like a lovely idea," Candace was quick to tell him. "In fact, a Scripture reading for staff members is such a good idea that maybe we should do it on a regular basis."

"Once will be enough if I'm the reader," he said. "Well, off to work." He wiped his mouth with a napkin then crumpled it. "I'm assisting on a gall bladder this morning."

"See you this afternoon," she called out, as he made his retreat.

It wasn't his assignment as surgical nurse that made James eager to get to his floor. He just didn't want to think about his practice session in the chapel. How many people had Elena invited? She was such an energetic organizer that she might fill the place. He could imagine her recruiting visitors and even ambulatory patients to be sure he had a big audience.

Would it help? He had his doubts. More likely, he would stammer and stutter his way through the verses until everyone in the chapel felt sorry for him. Worse, if he started stuttering again, would he be able to stop? Would all his conversation be stilted and painful because his old problem had returned to torment him?

He got onto the elevator, too wrapped up in his worries to notice someone else was in it.

"You look like you're snowed under with worries," a voice behind him said.

He turned to see Anabelle looking at him with a solicitous expression.

"Fern hasn't taken a turn for the worse, I hope."

"No, she's been pretty upbeat lately," he was happy to report. "Guess I was just thinking about what I have to do today."

"That wouldn't include a certain reading being held in the chapel, would it?" she asked, looking at him over the top of the glasses perched low on her nose.

He shrugged. Anabelle was a good friend, but he didn't want her to think he was obsessing over a few minutes of reading. She was responsible for getting him on the schedule at church, but he had no intention of laying a guilt trip on her if it went badly. He could have said no. He fervently wished he had said no. She wasn't to blame for wanting to help him.

James checked in at the nurses' station, welcoming the busy day ahead because it wouldn't give him much time to worry about the reading. He'd gone over the Bible verses so many times that he practically had them memorized. There was nothing more he could do except pray that his stuttering really was cured.

"James, you haven't forgotten about this afternoon, have you?" Elena came up beside him looking altogether too fresh and perky for this time of day. She was probably the only one on the hospital staff who ironed her scrubs.

"How could I? If perchance I somehow did, it seems you'd be quite happy to remind me."

"I think you'll have a nice crowd. Penny insisted on putting it on her calendar, and you know how she is."

"Yes," he said in a gloomy voice. "Everyone in the hospital will know about it."

"Remember, they're all your friends," she said, turning to leave.

"My friends," he said under his breath. Somehow, that was no help at all.

He prayed silently for the Lord's help in getting through this day, then exerted all his mental strength to concentrate on nothing but his work and the welfare of his patients.

Later he could worry about the chapel. Maybe by then, the knot of tension in his stomach would dissolve.

Chapter Twenty-One

JAMES TRIED TO THINK OF OTHER TIMES IN HIS life when he'd been filled with as much dread as he felt today. Certainly he'd been apprehensive when he shipped out for the Gulf War. Waiting to hear the diagnosis on Fern's MS had been even worse because someone he dearly loved was suffering.

In these situations, the quality of life and life itself was at stake. He'd drawn on his faith to get him through the rough times then, and certainly he could now.

He knew that reading a few verses was a trivial matter compared to the many critical situations he'd had to deal with in his job, but he'd also seen otherwise courageous people brought low by small things. He remembered the courage of an elderly man riddled with cancer whose spirit was broken because no one in his family wanted to adopt his aging cocker spaniel. A neighbor took the pet, but the patient lost heart because he felt that his family had let him down.

James had been haunted his whole life by the fear that his stuttering would return, and now it actually might. He knew his family wouldn't love him less, and his friends would be supportive. He wouldn't lose his job or the respect of the doctors and other staff members. At worst, he'd have to go back to speech therapy, and a medical professional should be willing to take advantage of help when it was necessary.

In short, there was no good reason for his apprehension. Somehow, that made his fear even harder to accept. He was a grown man in his fifties, and in his own mind he was being childish. He remembered another incident at Sunday school when the teacher had called on him to read a verse. He had tried to protest, but the teacher encouraged him, and so he stood. It was a replay of what had happened before—after much stammering, the teacher told him he didn't have to finish.

"Is it bad news?" A slender, gray-haired woman standing in front of her husband's room stopped him as he came down the corridor. "Tell me the truth. I can't stand not knowing."

"Didn't the doctor talk to you?" he asked.

"Yes, of course, he painted a rosy picture, but you look so worried. I thought maybe you were coming to tell me my husband's tests came back positive. I was afraid—"

"No, no," James quickly reassured her. "I'm sure the doctor told you everything there is to know. Your husband will be fine. He just needs to alter his lifestyle a little."

"Oh, I'll certainly see that he does that," she said with relief. "Thank you so much."

James watched her go back into the room, ashamed of himself for looking so glum that he alarmed a patient's spouse. He always tried to be upbeat and encouraging, but apparently he was failing miserably today, just as he expected to fail when he read.

He had less than two hours until he was due in the chapel.

Time flew by, and Elena caught up with him after they'd both signed out for the day.

"Ready?" she asked.

"No, but let's just get this over with."

They weren't the first to reach the chapel. In fact, every seat seemed to be occupied, and there was a low murmur of anticipation as he carried his Bible to the front of the room.

He tried not to see individuals as he passed them, but all his senses were especially acute. He was grateful to see Candace and Anabelle sitting together in the front row. If he looked up, at least he'd see friendly faces close to him. Right behind them, Penny Risser was seated with her arms folded across her chest, a challenging posture if he'd ever seen one. As he stepped up to the podium, he saw Albert Varner standing at the rear, arms crossed as though aping Penny. Why on earth had the hospital administrator bothered to come? This whole gathering was a much bigger deal than he'd anticipated, and it did nothing to steady his nerves.

The hospital chaplain, the Reverend Thomas Wiltshire, was standing beside the CEO, and James had to wonder whether the ordained minister thought he was overstepping his bounds by reading without his permission. For all he knew, though, Elena might have cleared it with the cleric before she corralled an audience for him.

His palms were damp, and he was afraid his voice would fail him before he even began.

Elena took it upon herself to introduce him, although everyone there knew him.

"James had the wonderful idea of gathering together a few staff members for a Bible reading," she said. "Sometimes in our busy lives, it's good to consider the words of the Lord and remember why we're here at Hope Haven."

He wanted to interrupt and say it hadn't been his idea, but he did have to accept the blame for everyone being there. If he hadn't been so nervous about reading in church, Elena never would have thought of asking people to come to the chapel to hear him.

"The reading today is from I Corinthians, chapter thirteen," he said, holding the Bible in front of him in both hands and clearing his throat to begin reading.

But before he started, it occurred to him to say a few words about the passage.

"Of all the inspired verses in the Bible, I think this chapter gives the clearest picture of what the role of love should mean in our lives."

He heard soft stirrings in the crowd and hoped he hadn't overreached himself by attempting to interpret what he was about to read.

Love is patient, love is kind, he thought, realizing that he really wanted to give this message to everyone assembled before him.

Suddenly he knew this wasn't about him. For whatever reason, he'd been given an opportunity to remind people how important love really was in their jobs, in their personal lives, and in their journey of faith.

The Bible fell open at the place he'd marked, and he began reading:

"If I speak in the tongues of men and of angels, but have not love, I am only a resounding gong or a clanging symbol. If I have the gift of prophecy and can fathom all mysteries and all knowledge, and if I have a faith that can move mountains, but have not love, I am nothing."

As he read, the meaning of the words gave him strength. He forgot all his concerns and doubts and let the message spill out of him without reservations. He didn't even remember the fear that had tormented him for days.

"And now these three remain: faith, hope and love. But the greatest of these is love."

He closed the book and bowed his head for a silent prayer of thanksgiving. He'd read all thirteen verses without a moment's hesitation. All his fears about stuttering had been for nothing. He hadn't stumbled over a single word. Now he knew he could read in church and give his presentation in Wisconsin without being plagued by doubt. The Lord had truly been with him today.

The people assembled in the chapel were silent. He hadn't expected applause—it wouldn't have been a proper response—but no one moved. No one seemed eager to go home after a long day's work. There wasn't even a cough or a whisper to be heard.

Were they waiting for him to dismiss them? How could he possibly add anything to the words of Paul?

"Paul of Tarsus was addressing these words to the church he founded in Corinth, Greece," he said, realizing that the people were expecting more from him. "It's about the love Christians should have for everyone, to love your neighbor as yourself. We all know how hard that is sometimes, but Hope Haven Hospital was founded on the principal of service to others. For myself, I'm very glad to be part of this long tradition and the love behind it. I thank you all for coming here today."

Elena stood up to add something, but she didn't have a chance. From the back of the room, Albert Varner spoke up, commanding everyone's attention.

"Thank you, James, for reminding all of us why we're here."

James glanced at his friends in the front row and was gratified to see Anabelle beaming at him. Candace looked far happier than when he'd left her in the cafeteria this morning, and Elena had a little grin of satisfaction. He loved them all, his close friends and all the people who'd come to support him.

Candace lingered behind when people left the chapel. She closed her eyes for a few moments of silent prayer. When she opened them, she looked up into the concerned face of Pastor Tom.

"How is everything going?" he asked in a kind voice.

She contemplated telling him everything was fine, but something in her heart prompted her to speak. "I should be doing better than I am," she admitted. Pastor Tom stared at her intently and gave her as much time as she needed to continue. She avoided his gaze and instead looked at her ring finger. "I just can't seem to get beyond my grief, even after almost four years. My support group helps, my friends are understanding, and my mother is wonderfully supportive. But I feel that I'm letting them all down." She met his kind eyes. "That I'm letting myself down too."

"There's no timetable for grief," the pastor said, sitting down beside her. "My grandmother used to say that time heals all."

"But I'm a committed Christian. I should have enough faith to accept Dean's death and move on."

"You have moved on in a way by caring for your children and helping to bring others into the world," he said in a soothing voice.

"I guess I'm just waiting to feel content again."

"Remember that God always answers prayers. He'll provide strength and peace of mind."

She was quiet for several moments, then responded with a small smile. "Maybe what I need is patience. Dean always said that I wanted today to be tomorrow."

The pastor took her hand in his and bowed his head, quietly asking God to heal her heart and fill it with joyful memories of her time with Dean.

Driving home, Candace could think of nothing but his words. In a sense she was already bringing happy memories together and sharing them with her children. She'd thought of the memory books as something she was doing for her children. Now she saw how important they were for her.

Elena was happy for James and grateful for the brief respite from her own worries, but as soon as she got to her car, the bad feelings returned. Where did faith figure in to her reaction to the hospital's land? She was so suspicious of the politician's intentions that it was causing great worry in her heart. She'd only recently come back to the church and she still had much to learn. Was there anything in His teachings to guide her in this dilemma? Was there an answer in the Bible? Her current hopes rested on Cesar's learning something incriminating.

No one was home when she got there. Rafael had left a note on the kitchen counter saying that he and Izzy were going to look for the new shoes she needed for spring. Cesar wasn't due home from basketball for another hour or so, giving her time to relax before she started dinner.

She put her soiled scrubs in the hamper and took a long shower, hoping it would calm her, but she couldn't get those two men out of her mind. They'd looked so smug and self-satisfied. It would be wrong if they used the hospital's inheritance for their own ends.

Cesar would be home soon, and no doubt he'd be hungry. She went to the kitchen and realized she hadn't given a thought to their dinner. Her mind had been too full of other things to do any meal planning. She was staring into the freezer compartment of the fridge, hoping for inspiration, when the kitchen door flew open and her husband burst into the room.

"Forget about cooking dinner," he said, whirling her around in a big bear hug. "We're going out to celebrate."

"Celebrate?" she asked a little breathlessly. "What do we have to celebrate?"

"I have the most beautiful wife in the world. Isn't that reason enough for a special meal?"

"Don't tease," she said swatting him. "Why are you so happy?"

"I've . . ." Cesar dragged out the word to build anticipation.

"You've . . . ," Elena encouraged.

"I've been called back to work!"

Elena squealed and hopped up and down. "Cesar, how wonderful! How did this happen?"

"O'Hanlon persuaded two guys close to retirement to step down a little early by offering their full pensions. They were only holding desk jobs, and O'Hanlon needed detectives, so two of us got called back. I wish I could say that everyone who was laid off was as lucky."

She hugged him. "I'll pray that all the officers will be called back soon. When can you leave your security job?"

"I have to work Saturday, but I've lined up one of the out-of-work cops to take over tonight and Sunday. He was glad to get the job, and I can't tell you how happy I am to be nearly done with guarding granite. Now go put on some pretty clothes."

"I'll just leave something for Izzy and Rafael's supper."

"Rafael can cook. I want to make an evening of it tonight because I still have to do the night shift tomorrow. My replacement has plans he can't break."

Elena forgot about her problems at work as she dressed in her best black dress and added a shimmering silver necklace that Cesar had given her some years ago. He put on a sports coat for the celebration and phoned for a reservation at Heritage House, a restaurant that claimed Abraham Lincoln had stopped there when he was a young lawyer, and the dwelling was still a private home.

The restaurant occupied the main floor of a house that was more than old enough to have hosted the young Lincoln. The rooms were small and intimate, and Elena was pleased to be seated in an old-fashioned parlor with a fireplace, the wood-burning grate now replaced by a gas burner. She didn't know whether the flocked red wallpaper and waxed wooden floorboards were authentic, but the gleaming white linen tablecloths and array of glassware at each place setting were certainly inviting.

"Are you sure we can afford this?" she whispered after a courteous young man in a burgundy jacket took their orders for blackened swordfish and trout almandine with wild rice.

"Nothing is too much for my Elena," Cesar said. "There's something else I want to discuss with you."

Elena felt a spike of alarm. Was this lovely dinner a way to prepare her for news she wouldn't like?

"I've been looking into the suggestion James made about taking online courses. It would be for when I retire from the police force. I love working with kids. That's the one good thing that came out of this layoff. If I start now, I may be close to getting a teaching certificate when I retire. That way, I can coach or be a classroom teacher, or maybe both."

Elena's cheeks strained, she couldn't smile any wider. She had to restrain herself from standing and announcing to the other patrons how proud she was of her husband. "I think that's a wonderful idea." She reached across the table and took his hand, her spirits soaring.

The years seemed to fall away as they quietly ate their dinner. They lingered over coffee, and Elena felt she had to ask the question that had been at the back of her mind throughout the lovely evening.

"Now that you're going back to work, will you be able to find out more about Leonard Baxter?"

"Are you sure you want to get involved in it?" he asked, frowning for the first time since making his big announcement.

"No, but I may be the one most concerned about their motives. You know Hope Haven means more to me than just a job."

Cesar leaned back in the captain's chair and folded his napkin beside his cup and saucer.

"If you really feel that strongly about it, I'll see what I can dig up, but don't be disappointed if there's nothing incriminating."

"There will be," Elena said, clenching her fists in her lap. "I feel so sure of it."

Her husband smiled indulgently, an expression she knew only too well.

"You think I'm overreacting," she said, "but I'm not."

The evening had been wonderful, a long overdue date for just the two of them, and Elena thanked the Lord that Cesar could go back to the work he did best. She was genuinely happy for the sake of her husband and their family, but concern about the hospital land still nagged at her. As much as Hope Haven could use the funds to update the care available to patients, she didn't want the land to be sold to people who didn't care about the hospital or the community. She prayed that the Lord would show her what to do if Cesar discovered anything damaging.

Chapter Twenty-Two

HOWIE WAS THRILLED. HE WAS INVITED TO A birthday party Saturday afternoon, and he could hardly wait. Fortunately, he was his usual healthy spirited self, so Candace wouldn't have to keep him home. In fact, he'd gone back to school yesterday and had come home talking a blue streak about what his friend Sammy was planning for his party.

They'd gone together to buy a gift, but it proved to be a lot harder than Candace could have imagined. Brooke's friends had always been pleased with Barbie accessories, books, or something pretty to wear. Sammy, on the other hand, only played with electronic games, at least according to Howie. She was completely at a loss to know what to get, especially when all the games seemed too complicated or too violent for a six-year-old.

Howie fixated on a game that featured a fire-breathing dragon about to consume a tiny human figure, but Candace firmly vetoed it.

"We don't know what kind of games Sammy's allowed to play or what kind will work at his house," she patiently explained.

"I know he'd like that one," Howie insisted.

She steered him to other toys for boys: metal trucks, board games, even a basketball, but Howie resisted all her suggestions.

"That's not what he likes," he insisted.

Candace had trudged through the superstore from one end to the next, and it was clear that her son would never agree on anything she pointed out, not even toys he might like for himself.

"Tell you what," she said. "Let's buy him a gift card, then he can come here and pick out something himself."

Howie was skeptical, but finally she convinced him that the plastic card was a good gift. It was that or leave the store without anything, and he was insistent that not be a possibility. He had to have a present to take to the party.

When did picking out a toy become so complicated? She usually enjoyed shopping for her own children.

She was happy to find a shelf full of scrapbooks and photo albums, including some that would make very nice memory books for her children. Howie picked one with a dark green cover and gold embossing. She found a similar one with a deep red cover for Brooke. Now each could have their own collection of mementos, and she was sure they had enough photos to do all three books.

"Can I start making it when we get home?" Howie asked, finally distracted from the problem of the gift.

"There won't be time. It's taken too long to do our shopping, but you can work on it tomorrow afternoon."

"Will you watch me?"

"Sure, I'll be happy to."

When they got home, Janet and Brooke had made plans of their own.

"We're going to the library," her mother said. "Brooke just discovered she has an overdue book. Then I'm dropping her off at Kenya's house, if you don't mind."

"No, that's fine," Candace agreed, although she had hoped to spend the afternoon with her daughter, perhaps working on the new scrapbook she'd just bought.

"We'll drop Howie at his party on the way," Janet said matter-of-factly.

"That would be nice of you. I'll pick him up after the party, though."

She didn't want to miss her son's excited account of what went on at the birthday party. She knew from experience that once he spilled out everything that interested him, he didn't like to tell it all again. It was one of the things she missed most when he got home from school before she got home from work. By the time he settled down to play in his room, he didn't have much to say.

They had homemade chicken noodle soup for lunch, left over from what her mother had made for supper last night. Then the kids and her mother got ready for their afternoon activities.

When they left, Candace felt at loose ends. Surely there were many jobs to do around the house, but she couldn't focus on anything. This was an ideal opportunity for some alone time, perhaps to read or clean a drawer, but she couldn't muster any enthusiasm. Of course, she could work on the memory book, but it wouldn't be the same doing it by herself. Brooke and

Howie's involvement made it seem so much more worthwhile, maybe because memories were more meaningful when they were shared.

She felt vaguely ashamed. Her children didn't deserve a mother who moped around feeling sorry for herself. Instead she should count her blessings, especially the love of her children and her mother. Compared to someone like Millie, who had no one in her life and no hope for the future, she was indeed fortunate.

Her week had been so busy that she hadn't made time to visit the homeless woman. Now she knew what to do with her spare time until her family came home.

The hospital seemed unusually quiet when she went in on the main floor. There were a few visitors, easily recognized when they carried flowers or other gifts, but certainly not enough to make the place seem busy. She peeked into the chapel, finding it empty, and remembered how happy she'd been when James did such a great job reading. Sometimes anticipating something scary was worse than facing it. She hoped she'd remember his example the next time she was challenged to do something difficult.

In fact, she was somewhat apprehensive about seeing Millie. She felt so helpless when it came to offering any kind of help. No doubt the patient's social worker had explored all her options, but there was no way to make up for not having family to care about her.

There had to be a better answer than the county home. Millie was too young to be institutionalized and too depressed to turn her life around on her own. The saddest thing was, she *did* have family. In Millie's mind, there were good reasons not to contact them, but how would they feel if they knew her situation?

Candace stepped onto the elevator, lugging a heavy sack of things she'd brought for Millie. She had nearly a week's worth of the *Deerford Dispatch* and some women's magazines her mother had finished. She'd also bought a few toiletries in a pretty flowered traveling kit, something Millie could use after she moved to the home.

The elevator stopped on Millie's floor, and Candace nearly collided with a man who was getting on.

"Sorry," he said in an absentminded voice, not looking away from the newspaper he was reading.

Looking at the elevator door as it closed, she was torn between annoyance and the germ of an idea. Most people read newspapers at least occasionally. A tiny news article buried in the middle of the paper had reported that a homeless woman had been found living in her car, but no relative had stepped forward as a result. What if she could get the paper to do a longer article on her? It was a long shot, but maybe it would flush out a relative or even a friend.

She walked slowly toward Millie's room, mulling over the idea. Her story was a sad one, but it wasn't news. The really interesting thing about Millie's life was the experience on the river with her grandfather. Stopping outside the door, Candace thought hard about the possibilities for a story. She was no reporter, but she remembered reading nostalgic stories featured in the local paper. People loved to read about their town's history, but unfortunately Deerford wasn't on the Mississippi. Would the

Dispatch use a story about Millie's grandfather based on the fact that she was a patient at Hope Haven?

Valera Kincaid was the person to call. Candace knew her casually because she was the reporter who covered hospital news for the paper. She was young, still in her midtwenties with bright red hair and freckles that made her look even younger, but what she lacked in experience, she more than made up for in enthusiasm.

How should she handle this? She didn't want to get Millie excited about a story unless it was a sure thing, but she might be moved to the county home at any time. Candace veered away from the open doorway, putting off her visit long enough to make a phone call in the visitor lounge, first looking up a number at the nurses' station.

Whatever she'd expected, it wasn't Valera Kincaid's promise to meet her there in an hour.

"You're a lifesaver," Valera said excitedly. "I'm supposed to have a local interest feature on my editor's desk by Monday, and the man who restores merry-go-round animals canceled our appointment to visit his sick brother. I've been at my wit's end trying to find something else, and this story sounds perfect. It has a great sense of American history, and I love doing my part to preserve those memories."

She said all this in one breath, leaving it to Candace to tell Millie she was coming.

"Of course, I'll need a good picture of the grandfather or his barge," Valera said. "If you can get one with your patient as a little girl, all the better."

Candace's heart sank. She had no idea whether such a picture existed, but she didn't tell the reporter not to come. Maybe, just maybe, Millie did have a picture of her grandfather.

Millie wasn't exactly excited about the prospect of telling the reporter about her grandfather, but she didn't offer any objections. Candace knew that talking about him was one of her few pleasures and hoped that the interview would go well in spite of her initial indifference.

"One thing, Millie," she said as the patient went through the bag of gifts, "Miss Kincaid will need a picture of your grandfather or his barge, one she can use in the newspaper. Do you have any?"

"I do, but they're in my car. My social worker said she'd have the stuff brought to me after I'm in the county home."

"Where is your car?"

"At the police impound lot. I guess that's where they take abandoned cars. It will be sold for scrap if I don't claim it pretty soon."

"If I can find it, where would the pictures be?"

"I had them in one of Granddad's old cigar boxes. I put it under the seat because it's the one thing I'd hate to have stolen."

"Do you mind if I try to find them?"

Millie slowly nodded her head. "I surely would like to see them again."

Candace raced out of the hospital with no clear idea of where to go. Would the police let her get to the car? Would she need some kind of authorization? She checked her watch and saw that she had a little over an hour before she had to pick up Howie. Regretfully, she called her mother's cell phone.

"Mom, could you possibly pick up Howie after the party?"

"Of course I'll go get him," Janet agreed. "What did you say you have to do?"

"I'll explain later, Mom. Thanks so much." She said goodbye with a twinge of regret for missing her son's firsthand report on the party.

She wasn't even sure where the police compound was, and the only policeman she knew was Elena's husband. She hated to bother him, especially since he might be sleeping before going to his night job, but this might be Millie's one chance for a new life.

Elena answered, and Candace explained the situation as quickly as she could.

"Cesar's sleeping," Elena said. "I would hate to wake him, but if it's really important—"

"Terribly important."

"Well, this is his last night guarding tombstones," Elena said in a happy voice. "Monday he goes back to work on the force. Hold on. I'll go ask him."

The wait seemed interminable, but at last Elena came back.

"He called a friend who's on duty. He'll meet you at the impound lot and open it for you."

"Oh, thank you, thank you. But I don't know where it is."

Candace had her repeat the directions twice, although she was familiar with the road. As she drove there, she tried to remember what the car looked like. She'd only seen it once, but how many abandoned cars could a town this size have?

The uniformed officer who met her outside the chain-link fence was middle-aged and muscular with clear blue eyes and a swagger in his stance. He introduced himself as Officer Marcus and unlocked the padlock on the gate.

Candace took one look and her heart sank. There were rows and rows of cars with muddy lanes between them.

"How can I find the one I need?"

"What's the license number?"

"I have no idea."

"Do you know the make and year?"

She shook her head, feeling her heart sink.

"What about the color?"

"It was faded and rusty, maybe once blue."

She wasn't even sure of that. It had been a snowy winter morning, not fully light, and she'd been in a hurry to get to work.

"There are some old wrecks over here," he said, leading the way.

"It wasn't in an accident, not a serious one anyway. As I remember, it was just old. And I'm sure it was bigger than modern cars."

She followed after the officer, ignoring the mud that seeped through the thin layer of gravel and caked on her boots.

They walked all the way to the far fence, and nothing looked even remotely familiar.

"Where do all these cars come from?" she asked, straining to keep up with his pace.

"They accumulated over the winter. I imagine we'll be having an auction this summer if there are any worth more than scrap."

He was passing a sporty red car that looked as if it had lost an argument with a semi. As a nurse, Candace could imagine the horrible injuries that people must have sustained in some of the wrecks. She didn't like this place at all, but a nondescript old vehicle one lane over caught her eye.

"That could be it," she said pointing.

She approached the car and opened a rear door, thankful that it wasn't locked. She'd never thought to ask Millie about the key.

Conscious of the policeman waiting for her, she poked her head into the car. The air inside was stale and unpleasant, and it made her want to cry that all Millie's possessions were crammed into the aging vehicle.

The box was supposed to be under a seat, so she tried the back first, coming up with wads of used tissues, candy wrappers, and other debris. She very much wanted to forget the whole thing, but instead she closed the back door and bent over the driver's seat. There she found an old pair of shoes, three pennies, and a plastic bag with mismatched knives, spoons, and forks.

With a sigh, she walked around to the passenger side, feeling slightly queasy from the musty odor. When she reached under the last seat, her hand touched something hard with the contours of a box. She tried to pull it out, tugging as hard as she could, but it was stuck.

"I think this is what I need, but I can't get it out," she said, appealing to the bored-looking policeman.

"Let me try."

Officer Marcus bent over the seat and pulled hard on the object. He was banging on the box with the handle of an old flashlight he'd found on the back seat, adding a few choice words to his efforts. At last it broke free and came into view on the floor in front of the seat.

Candace quickly picked it up and opened it, hoping Millie had remembered right. The box was full of paper including envelopes that looked like they contained bills. On the bottom there was a stack of photographs in a plastic Baggie. She pulled off her gloves and quickly sorted through them, smiling when she saw a picture of a little girl and an old man standing beside what could only be a river barge.

"I can't thank you enough," she said to the policeman. "You don't know how much these pictures mean to the owner."

"Glad to help you out," he said, slamming the car door and leading her toward the gate.

Would this cache help locate Millie's missing relatives? She found herself praying that it would.

Chapter Twenty-Three

THE BELL FAMILY WAS READY FOR CHURCH. FERN WAS wearing her favorite sweater, light blue cashmere with white flowers embroidered around the neck, and navy wool slacks. She looked even smaller than her five feet, and her loose-fitting clothes didn't disguise the fact that she was thinner than she used to be. But to her husband, she was still the beautiful pixie-faced girl he'd married over twenty years ago.

Her eyes were bright with excitement this morning, and she insisted on leaving the wheelchair at home.

"Springtime has finally come, meaning no snow or ice. I'll do just fine with the walker," she said. "Nelson, I don't care if you wear a hoodie, but please, not that awful gray one."

James smiled as his younger son went back to his room to find one that would satisfy his mother. An eighth grader, he was a mass of contradictions, sometimes so adult that his father swelled with pride and other times a rascal who would get away with whatever he could. Fortunately James remembered his own middle school experiences and knew that the rebellious years would pass.

Gideon, two years older and more serious than his younger brother, smirked, probably because he'd told Nelson that he couldn't get away with wearing the raggedy garment to church. He was wearing a brown wool sports jacket, his first foray into adult clothing, and even with jeans, it made him look considerably more mature than his brother.

When Nelson came back to the kitchen where they were waiting to leave, James glanced at his watch. They still had time to spare, and he had something to say to his boys.

"You know I'm reading in church this morning," he said.

"Nice," Gideon said, but his brother only raised one eyebrow, a trick he'd inherited from his father.

"I want to explain why I've never read before."

"Do you really want to—" Fern started to say.

"Yes, I think it's important they know." James gave her a gentle smile and continued. "When I was young, I had a stuttering problem."

"You don't stutter now," Gideon said, looking puzzled.

"No, I went to speech therapy for quite a while. I thought my problem was solved, but there was still a kernel of doubt in my mind." He gestured with his thumb and forefinger to indicate smallness.

"Anyway, I've always been afraid that it might come back. Fear kept me from speaking before a group, even to read from the Bible. But a good friend at work convinced me to practice reading before a group in the hospital chapel. And you know what?"

"What?" Nelson asked, pursing his lips as though he wasn't sure why his father was telling them this.

"I read, and I didn't stutter. All those years, I let a vague fear keep me from speaking in front of a group."

"I didn't think you were afraid of anything," Nelson said, sounding more confused than disappointed.

"There's nothing wrong with being afraid," James said, carefully weighing his words. "Faith pulls you through."

"Now your father is going to give a speech in Wisconsin this spring," Fern said happily. "About faith-based nursing and how to incorporate Christian principles into health care."

"And I have some news that even your mother hasn't heard."

"What would that be?" Fern asked, sounding a bit surprised.

"Somehow Mr. Varner heard about the conference—probably from Penny Risser. He thought it was such a good idea that he wants me to give my presentation at a staff meeting this week. It will be good practice for me, and hopefully it will be helpful to them."

"That's wonderful!" Fern said, reaching for his hand. "I'm so proud of you."

"I'll have a lot of work to do on it today and tomorrow, but now I'm sure I can stand up and testify to my faith without stuttering."

He smiled at his boys, and both of them grinned back.

"Now let's get to church," James said. "I can hardly believe it, but I'm actually excited about reading this morning."

Fern insisted on sitting in the front pew instead of their usual one. The boys grumbled a bit when she insisted they sit as a family instead of with their friends. James had to wipe his damp palms on his pants several times, but he felt a sense of calm when he remembered where he was. When he was called to read, he cleared his throat and adjusted the microphone, looking out at the faces he loved most.

The congregation was silent as he read. He felt his shoulders relaxing and his demeanor exuding more confidence as he eased into his new role. The absence of coughing, fidgeting, and whispering told him that it was well received, and he fervently thanked the Lord for letting him overcome his fear.

As he closed the Bible, he looked into Fern's face. Her moist eyes and the boys' grins of approval were the greatest accolade he could have had.

Elena shared a hasty breakfast with her husband on Monday morning. He was eager to get back to work, but she was too agitated to let him go without more reassurance.

"Are you sure that's all you can do?" she asked as she buttered a slice of toast.

"I told you, Baxter has never been in trouble. The worst I could find was some unpaid parking tickets. There's really no reason for you to get involved."

"Please don't lecture me, Cesar. You know how worried I am."

"Mr. Varner is a very smart man," her husband said. "I don't think he got to be head of the hospital without being able to read character. Have some faith in him."

"He's not the only one who cares about the hospital."

"Promise me you'll let this rest."

She looked directly into the dark eyes she loved and reluctantly nodded assent.

"Good enough." He quickly kissed her forehead and started pulling on his coat. "Now I have to hurry. You don't want me to be late on my first day back, do you?"

"Have a good day," she said, handing him his coffee-filled thermos. She was pleased to see him so happy but still wondered what Baxter and his friend might be up to.

When she arrived at the nurses' station, the nurse supervisor quickly filled her in on several patients who'd been admitted to Intensive Care over the weekend. Elena didn't have time to stew, but she still went through her day's work with a sense of unease. What plans were in the works for the hospital's land? She didn't have answers, but questions popped up every time she had a few free seconds.

A strip mall would be terrible for the downtown businesses, but there were even worse uses. Would the zoning board let the developer build an apartment complex that would alter the dynamic around the hospital? She'd even heard rumors about drag-racing in the area. She knew how noisy auto tracks were, certainly loud enough to disturb patients in the hospital.

"Why so gloomy?" Anabelle asked when they went into the cafeteria together for lunch.

"Oh, just fuming over—" She remembered her promise to Cesar, but did it apply to talking things over with a close friend? "It's nothing really," she said, her conscience deciding for her. "What's up with you?"

"Cameron is taking Sarge to obedience school. I don't know who's being trained, my husband or the dog. Anyway, my hand feels much better since I stopped walking him—the dog, not Cameron."

Elena chuckled at the thought of Cameron's going to doggy school and filled her tray with salad, sandwich, and vanilla pudding for dessert.

As the two nurses looked for an empty table, James waved at them.

"I hear you're going to give your conference presentation at the staff meeting tomorrow," Anabelle said.

"Good for you!" Elena said enthusiastically.

"I owe it all to you," he said, including them both. "If you hadn't insisted on a practice session in the chapel, I wouldn't have the confidence to do it."

"He read at church yesterday," Anabelle told Elena. "Did a wonderful job, but then, I knew he would."

His face went pink at the praise. Later, as the three started gathering their trash from lunch, Elena was proud she'd kept her promise to Cesar and had gotten through lunch without saying a word about the hospital land. Now she just had to finish her shift and go home.

Something was stirring on the main floor when she was leaving for home at the end of her shift. She didn't hear ambulance sirens as she would for a major disaster, but staff members were congregating in small groups instead of going home. There was a buzz in the air, and she was too curious to leave without finding out the reason.

One person always knew what was happening. Penny stepped out of an elevator and made a beeline for her office, but Elena was too quick for her. She blocked her way, although for a moment it seemed that the executive assistant would bowl her over.

"I have to—" Penny snapped, smoothing down the edges of her gray tweed jacket.

"Just stop a second, please," Elena said, trying not to sound as desperate for news as she was. "What's going on?"

"Six o'clock news," Penny barked, sidestepping to get around her. "I have to get back to the office."

"There must be more you can tell me," Elena said, but Penny only shook her head and scooted away.

The off-duty staff members were gradually moving toward the exit, their faces showing that they were as puzzled as she was. Someone had started a rumor, but no one had any concrete information. Elena headed home, eager to follow up on Penny's comment about the news. That was one broadcast she would be sure to tune in.

The news came on as she was making dinner, but she was able to turn down the oven and let the rice sit while she watched. Unfortunately, Isabel lay in front of the TV, engrossed in a cartoon.

"Izzy, honey, I'm sorry but Grandma has to watch the news." She changed the channel over her granddaughter's squeal of protest.

"That's my favorite show!"

"Whatever is on is your favorite show," she said, feeling a bit silly for squabbling over the television. "This is a really important newscast. Tell you what. Why don't you go get some of those chicken-shaped crackers, and we'll have a little snack before dinner."

Eating right before dinner was a no-no at their house, so naturally Izzy was happy to oblige. Elena had a twinge of conscience, but she had to know why Penny had told her to watch.

"Dinner nearly ready, Mom?" Rafael asked, poking his head into the room.

"Pretty soon. I told Izzy she could have some crackers." Elena perched on the arm of the sofa.

"Wow, whatever you're watching must be important. You never let me eat right before dinner," he teased.

She waved her arms and shushed him, turning her full attention to the pair of anchors going through the day's news. So far nothing had to do with the hospital.

"What's for dinner?" Cesar asked, coming into the room as the local news was winding down.

"Just a minute."

She missed the first few words, but caught the end of the short report: Leonard Baxter had withdrawn as a candidate in the upcoming election.

"Does that put your mind at ease?" her husband asked, bending down to kiss the top of her head.

". . . special meeting of the Hope Haven Hospital at seven this evening to announce plans for the land on . . ."

"That's it!" Elena cried out. "If they're going to sell to Baxter's crony, they'll announce it tonight. I want to be there to hear it."

"I'm sure you can hear it on the late news," Cesar said. "Don't you want to know how my first day back went?"

"Of course. How did it go?" she asked, giving him a quick kiss on the lips before hurrying toward the kitchen.

"Fine. Are you really going to that meeting?" he asked, following her.

"I certainly am. They didn't say anything about it being closed to the public."

"But dinner . . ."

At that moment, the timer went off.

"Ta-da! Ready," she said, turning the oven off. "Put the leftovers in the fridge. I'll eat later."

"You can't stop them, no matter what the decision."

"I know, but I'm too agitated to eat. The rice is done, the chicken's in the oven, and there's a salad in the fridge. I want to get there early in case there's a big crowd."

Elena didn't know what she planned to do if Baxter and his friend got the land. What she couldn't do was sit home and wait to hear. For better or worse, she had to be at the hospital when the announcement was made.

When she got there, the boardroom wasn't as crowded as she'd expected, but there was a TV cameraman and a reporter she recognized from the *Deerford Dispatch.* The board members weren't there yet, but there was an expectant hush as a handful of spectators waited for the announcement.

"What do you think?" a soft voice said close to her ear.

"Anabelle! I didn't expect to see you here."

"I actually came to visit a friend who had her appendix out, but as long as I was here—well, I'm as curious as anyone."

The board members started coming to their places at the long table, not speaking to each other or anyone else. Albert Varner was the last to arrive, taking the place at the head of the table usually reserved for the president.

"Ladies and gentlemen," he said, "if I may have your attention, please."

The murmuring quieted down, and the TV cameraman moved closer.

"The governing board of Hope Haven has asked me to announce the sale of the land recently left to the hospital. Before her death, our benefactor, Mrs. Jantz, had several offers to buy the land. It was her will that the hospital board make the decision after she passed away, based on what would be best for Hope Haven and Deerford. It has been a difficult decision, but the board unanimously agrees that the property doesn't fit into plans for future expansion of the hospital. The proceeds from the sale will be used to update the technology and the level of service we can offer our patients and the community."

Elena dug her nails into her palms and wished he'd get on with it. Did this mean Baxter had won, in spite of his withdrawal from the election? She desperately wanted to ask, but the hospital CEO was still talking.

"Our decision ultimately came down to two offers and we considered both of them very seriously. After much discussion, the board didn't feel that commercial development on the site would be in the best interests of Hope Haven or the community." Varner paused and looked down at his papers, then looked up again. "For that reason, the board has agreed to sell the land to the Heartwood Corporation for the purpose of building an assisted-living facility. When completed, it will allow our seniors to stay in their own community and have access to the level of care that they need. I'm very proud to welcome the Heartwood development to Deerford."

Elena was so relieved she could hardly believe it. There was enthusiastic applause from everyone in the room, and the cameraman moved in for a closer shot.

"Isn't that splendid?" Anabelle whispered beside her. "People have been talking about the need for good senior housing for ages. Now it's going to become a reality."

At the front of the room, Mr. Varner was answering questions and receiving congratulations. Elena wanted to join them, but even more, she wanted to hurry home and tell Cesar the wonderful news.

"I have to go now," she said, impulsively hugging Anabelle.

All the way home, she thanked God for the wonderful news and for the good sense of the hospital administrator and the board. The Lord did work in mysterious ways.

Chapter Twenty-Four

CANDACE NEEDED TO PICK UP A FEW THINGS AT THE supermarket on her way home from work Tuesday, making her a little later than usual. She was eager to see whether the young reporter had made good on her promise to tell Millie's story in the *Dispatch*. It hadn't been in Monday's paper, and Candace was a little worried that the interview hadn't gone well. Or possibly the editor had decided not to use the story after it was written.

She didn't see the newspaper lying near the front door as it usually was by this time. Hopefully this wouldn't be the one day of the year that the carrier forgot to leave one.

When she brought the bag of groceries into the kitchen, her mother was sitting at the table reading the front page.

"Isn't this wonderful news?" Janet said. "I've been on the phone all day. My friends are delighted that the town is going to have its own assisted-living facility. And so close to the hospital too. Madge's mother lives over forty miles away, and she wants to get her mother's name on the list right away. She'd love to have her mother closer and is worn out from all the driving to visit her. Maybe I should put my name on the waiting list for when I need it."

"Mom! You have a home with us." Candace was shocked that her mother would think of living anywhere else.

"But if the time ever comes—"

"You're healthy as a thirty-year-old. We don't need to think about that now."

Janet smiled and didn't say anything else.

"Have you seen the article about our homeless woman?" Candace asked.

"No, I haven't gotten beyond the front page, but you can have the paper. I'll read the rest later."

Candace immediately started thumbing through the front section and found it tucked away on the last page.

"Homeless Woman Reminisces about Life on the Mississippi."

Millie hadn't exactly lived on the river, but Candace was willing to forgive the exaggeration. Valera Kincaid had used not one but three pictures of the barge, the captain, and Millie as a child. It was truly amazing what Millie remembered about navigating the treacherous Mississippi, considering how young she'd been. She'd given a vivid picture of eating, sleeping, and working on the barge. The young reporter had captured Millie's regard for her grandfather as well as her excitement at making the trip with him.

"Is it a good article?" Janet asked.

"Marvelous! I just hope someone who knows Millie will see it. Her only real hope for a better life is to connect with someone close who will help her."

"Mom!" Brooke called out as she dashed up from the lower level. "I want you to see my memory book. It's nearly done."

Her daughter had worked diligently on her own book and the big memory book, turning down an invitation to a friend's house Sunday afternoon to keep working. She'd even been reasonably tolerant of Howie's efforts, helping him when his hands were too sticky from the glue to handle photographs.

Candace followed her daughter down to the lower level and opened the book she'd made for herself. Nothing had prepared her for the latest addition to Brooke's book. She'd carefully sketched a deep blue river running through page after page with colored pencils. It had been a time-consuming effort, and she'd even included fish in the water and birds in the sky. Candace was so touched by the way her daughter incorporated the river theme that it was hard to hold back tears.

"It's wonderful," she said, turning the pages and seeing how much effort Brooke had put into it.

"I wonder whether I should do the same in the big book," she said, meaning the first one they'd started.

"What do you think? It's certainly a lovely idea, but it will take a lot of time."

"No problem. I don't have any homework tonight. I finished it all in school so l can have my evening free."

"Do whatever you think would be nice," Candace said, more than willing to let Brooke use her creativity in any way she saw fit.

She still marveled at how much her daughter loved doing the memory book. Certainly it was bringing her closer to her father, at the same time turning her grief into pride in his accomplishments. Candace felt less despondent because her children were accepting Dean's death and remembering him with affection. The project had succeeded beyond her expectations. She still greatly regretted that Dean had been taken away from them while his family still needed him so much, but it brought her far more comfort than she'd ever imagined to be able to relive all their joyful times through the memory books.

Usually Candace struggled to keep a positive attitude both at home and at work, but Wednesday morning she didn't have that familiar urge to stay in bed and hide under the covers. True, it was still a strain—being cheerful and upbeat for her family, her co-workers, and her patients—but she didn't feel an overwhelming urge to give herself over to mourning as she sometimes did when she first woke up. She was excited to think about sharing the news with Lila and the group at the next meeting.

When she reached the Birthing Unit, there was a heightened sense of urgency that usually preceded a difficult birth. Two doctors were conferring outside a delivery room, an OB/GYN who frequently had patients at Hope Haven and an older man she didn't recognize. Riley hurried out of the room and spoke to the two doctors, then came up to Candace.

"Twins," she said. "The mother's been in labor since midnight. We don't know yet whether she'll need a C-section. It's her second pregnancy."

Something happened to Candace whenever she was confronted with a medical emergency or a crisis in the Birthing

Unit. She was able to put aside concerns about her family and her lingering grief for Dean and give herself up completely to the needs of the moment.

Her day became even more hectic when a woman came in with false labor pains, and the husband of another expectant mother demanded more attention than his wife did. The lunch break came and went, and the situation got worse when one of the young RNs had to go home with a migraine.

At 2:17 PM, twin boys were born without a C-section, arriving in the world with high-pitched howls. Their birth weight was healthy, and their mother was thrilled, though exhausted.

"We're going to name them Joshua and Dean after their two grandfathers," she said when she held them for the first time.

Candace had a difficult moment when she heard her husband's name, but she quickly rallied. A healthy baby was always a cause for joy, doubly so with twins.

She was tired and hungry, but the satisfaction of helping bring new life into the world more than compensated for her discomfort. She signed out for the day with only one thought in mind: going home.

Anabelle caught up with her as she went to get her coat.

"You're staying for James's presentation, aren't you?" she asked.

"Oh dear, I forgot. Yes, of course I will. I'll have to call my mother and let her know."

"Want me to save you a seat?"

"Yes, please."

The call to her mother only took a minute, but she remembered something else she had to do before the staff meeting.

She wanted to know what Millie thought about the newspaper article.

The door was open, but Millie wasn't in the room. Her bed was neatly made up, but there was no sign that she'd ever been in there. Her few personal possessions were gone.

Candace felt sick at heart, believing that the homeless woman had been moved to the county home.

"She left," a voice said from the other bed.

A tiny little woman with a halo of snow-white hair rose up on one elbow to talk to her.

"Do you know where she went?"

"Can't say, but a woman came and got her. Tall, thin with black hair—well, mostly black. Could have been some gray. My eyes aren't what they used to be."

"Well, thank you," Candace said, going back to the corridor to see if one of the staff could tell her more.

An LPN was coming down the hallway, and Candace intercepted her.

"Do you know where Millie went, the homeless woman with diabetes complications?" she asked.

"Sorry, hon, I just came on. Didn't even know she'd left."

After asking another nurse, Candace gave up. Maybe tomorrow she could confirm Millie's location, but now she had to hurry so she wouldn't miss any of her friend's presentation.

Penny had scheduled the community health room for James's talk, and she was standing outside the door like a majordomo, making sure everyone hustled to take a seat. The staff meetings focused on in-service education and were optional, although everyone who worked directly with patients was encouraged to attend if they could. Candace was conscientious about any type of professional growth, but she was especially excited to hear what James had to say.

He was standing at the front of the room by a portable chalkboard, waiting for his audience to settle down. She would never have guessed that he'd ever had any reservations about public speaking. He looked calm and fully in control of the situation. In fact, she detected a small smile, as though he had a secret.

"Staff members and friends, thank you for taking time from your busy schedules to come here today."

James launched right into his talk, and Candace was immediately interested, sensing that those around here were too.

"It's not our job to convert patients or force our beliefs on them," James said, "but we've all seen the power of God at work in the most difficult of times. By administering to our patients with love and giving them emotional help as well as medical care, we're integrating spirituality and medical science. Hope Haven was founded on this principle, but it's up to you, the caregivers, to give the support patients need."

Candace agreed with all that James said, but as she listened, she wondered whether she'd done all she could to provide faith-based care. For too long she'd allowed grief to undermine the strength of her beliefs. Had that made her less effective in her job? Was she less of a caregiver when she hadn't resolved her emotional turmoil? Was her relationship with her family, friends, and patients tainted by her grief? James seemed to be speaking directly to her.

The audience applauded when James finished, as well they might. He'd given a wonderful presentation, and only his close friends knew how hard he had struggled to overcome his fear.

"Didn't he do an outstanding job?" Anabelle asked, clapping along with the others.

"Yes, he certainly did," Candace agreed, feeling genuinely upbeat, thanks to his words.

She congratulated James, then left as quickly as she could, passing up the trays full of cookies that Penny had personally baked for the occasion. There was a woman who was full of contradictions. She could be outspoken, even harsh, in her dealing with the staff, but she must have spent countless hours making treats. Did she do so out of love or for the praise her fancy goodies brought? Or was it because the hospital was her whole life and the staff members were her surrogate children?

Thank You, Lord, for my family and friends. I don't know what I'd do without them, she silently prayed as she left the building and headed for home.

Chapter Twenty-Five

Candace couldn't remember when her workweek had seemed so long, but at last her Friday shift was nearly over.

"You ready for the weekend?" Riley asked, coming up beside her at the nurses' station.

"It's been a long week," Candace said with a slight smile.

"That it has," the nurse supervisor agreed. "A friend of mine raises sheep. One year she lost one of her ewes giving birth, so she took the lamb into her home and bottle-fed it until it could survive with the rest of the flock. When our spring babies are born, I always think about the little nest she made for it in her kitchen. Sometimes little ones need extra special care. That keeps me coming to work even when I'm bone tired and tempted to stay home."

Candace felt as though she'd received a gift. It wasn't like Riley to be sentimental, and she rarely shared personal stories.

"Oh, I nearly forgot," Riley went on. "Penny Risser sent up a message for you. She wants you to stop in her office before you leave for the day."

"Okay, I will," Candace agreed, although she couldn't imagine why the executive assistant would want to see her.

After work she picked up her coat and purse before going down to the main floor, still puzzled about Penny's request.

The office door was ajar, and she walked up to the desk, waiting a few minutes while Penny argued with someone on the phone. She sounded especially cross.

Candace hoped she wasn't in some kind of trouble, although she couldn't imagine what she'd done wrong.

"Candace, sorry to make you wait," Penny said after cutting off her caller and hanging up the phone none too gently. "I have a letter here that must be for you."

She held out a small white envelope addressed to Nurse Candace at the Hope Haven Hospital.

"There's no return address," Penny pointed out, obviously waiting for her to open it and satisfy her curiosity.

Her first instinct was to put the letter in her purse and read it later, but there was no reason to keep it a secret. After all, if it was a personal message, it would have gone to her home address.

"I have a letter opener," Penny said, handing her a knife with an ornate metal handle. "Mr. Varner gave it to me last Christmas."

"It's very nice," Candace said, carefully slitting open the top of the envelope.

The note inside was written on a sheet of lined paper torn from a spiral notebook. The handwriting wasn't familiar, but Candace sighed with relief when she read the message:

Dear Nurse Candace,

I'm sorry I didn't see you before I left. My sister-in-law came to get me. A friend of hers who lives in Deerford called her about the article. She said it was time for me and my brother to get over being mad. I'm going to live with them until I can get back on my feet. She is trying to get me a job helping at a day care center. I would really like that. Thank you for all you did for me. I'm still wearing that real nice coat even though it's getting warm. Thank you for praying for me and for being my friend.

Millie

Candace's eyes were moist when she finished reading the short note. Her first instinct was to hurry from the office so she could read the wonderful note again in the solitude of her car, but she didn't want to hurt Penny's feelings.

"It's from a patient—well, not my patient, exactly. The homeless woman with diabetes. Did you read the *Dispatch* article about her grandfather's Mississippi River barge? Someone called her sister-in-law about it, and she's gone to live with her and her brother."

"Well, it's nice to get a letter with good news," Penny said, as though she received bad news every time the mail carrier came.

"Thanks for holding this for me," she said.

If Penny was still trying to live up to her reputation as a hard-hearted administrator, she had been failing recently. Candace detected the hint of a smile on her face and real warmth in her eyes. But it was only a flash before she ushered Candace out of the office.

Hurrying out of the building, Candace nearly walked past Heath without seeing him.

"Candace, are you in a rush to leave? How about going over to the Corner with me for coffee? I feel we haven't had a chance to talk in a while."

Her first instinct was to say no, but she read the invitation in his eyes and didn't want to refuse. It suddenly occurred to her that she'd been avoiding him because she felt disloyal to Dean. If she truly wanted to move on, she had to be open to new friendships.

"I'd love to," she said, realizing that she meant it.

The small restaurant was relatively quiet, but for once Candace didn't care who saw them together.

"I saw the first robin of spring today," he said when they were seated.

"How wonderful. I think everyone has had more than enough winter this year."

"How about we celebrate the coming of spring? I'm all for a piece of pecan pie," he said with a twinkle in his eye.

"I haven't had the Corner's key lime pie in forever."

Heath ordered their pie and coffee, then shrugged out of his winter jacket. He was wearing a long-sleeved cotton knit shirt in a cheerful yellow color, and it raised her spirits even further to be near him.

"*Mmm*, delicious," she said as she took tiny bites to make the treat last—or maybe to prolong the pleasant time with Heath.

"What do you think of the board's decision to sell the land?" he asked as they sipped second cups of coffee.

"It's certainly welcome news, what with all the speculation of a strip mall or drag-racing track. Can you imagine? And my mom's friend is looking forward to not having to drive the forty miles each way to visit her mother."

"She may have to wait until they at least break ground," he said with a smile.

They lingered until Candace knew she should get home. This was easily the most enjoyable afternoon she'd had in a long time, and she thanked the Lord for the respite from sadness.

Rereading the letter in the car before she drove home, Candace found that the message hit home even harder. After all her suffering, Millie was reunited with family. Candace was more grateful than she would have thought possible. No matter how the reunion with her brother went, Millie wouldn't be alone anymore.

Turning into the driveway at home, she didn't feel nearly as tired as usual. In fact, Millie's letter had lifted her spirits more than she could have imagined, and sharing a treat with Heath was icing on the cake. When she stepped into the kitchen, the aroma of cinnamon assailed her nostrils. Her mother had been baking, and the counter was filled with cooling racks full of cookies.

"Goodness, it looks like Christmas around here," she teased as Janet took another pan from the oven.

"Howie needs treats for his class Monday, and I thought I'd send some to work with you. Don't know anyone who deserves homemade cookies more than hardworking nurses."

"You're an angel," Candace said, hugging her mother after she set the pan on top of the stove. "I don't know what I'd do without you."

"I'm the one who's blessed. Being here with you is like reliving the best part of my life, the years when I had children to raise."

"Mommy!" Howie called out as he raced into the room. "You have to come see our memory books."

"Just give me a minute to take off my coat," she said, smiling at her son's excitement.

He impatiently hopped from foot to foot while she hung it in the front closet, then led her down to the lower level.

Brooke was standing beside the old Ping-Pong table with the three books sitting side by side: the large leather-covered scrapbook and the two smaller ones.

"We're done," her daughter said with a happy smile.

"Look at mine first," Howie said, picking it up and handing it to Candace.

She sat between the two children on the old couch, turning page by page exclaiming over Howie's art and the way he had pasted in the photographs.

"Brooke helped me," he said. "I don't like it when my fingers get sticky."

"You did a wonderful job. I love this picture of Daddy with his golf club," Candace said, remembering how she'd wanted to take lessons so she was good enough to play with him.

Brooke showed amazing patience as she waited for Howie to talk about every page in his book, but at last it was her turn.

Candace had already seen most of her daughter's pages, but they went through the whole book.

"I don't remember this Christmas," Brooke said a bit sadly as they looked at a picture of Dean holding her in front of the decorated tree.

"You were only two," her mother said, feeling a lump in her throat at the memory of Brooke as an angel in the church Christmas pageant.

Both she and Dean had been sure their daughter would either cry or wander away from the manger group, but she'd been absolutely perfect in her little white robe and slightly crooked halo.

Candace was nearly overwhelmed by memories as Brooke proudly turned the pages of her book. She wanted to weep over the happiness she'd shared with her husband. For the sake of the children, she managed to make positive comments without breaking down. The memory books were terribly important to the children, but they were also helping her deal with her grief in ways she couldn't have anticipated. They represented what she had been given, not what had been taken away.

"Now for the real surprise," Brooke said, putting aside her book and getting the big book from the table. "You haven't seen my river."

True to her word, Brooke had painstakingly drawn a stream of blue on every page, carefully making it line up from page to page. She put in whimsical touches like a little boy fishing and a small boat as well as fish and birds. The river skirted around photographs and other mementos, never intrusive but skillfully pulling all the pages together.

"You've done an absolutely wonderful job."

"I did too, Mommy," Howie reminded her.

"Yes, you certainly did," she said, hugging him close.

"You haven't seen the end," Brooke said, slowly turning the last few pages. "Rivers have to go someplace."

She turned the last page very slowly, an artist unveiling her masterpiece. Candace smiled at the dramatic touch until she saw what her wise daughter had done on the last page.

There were no photographs, only the river widened to cover almost the whole width of the page. At the bottom, in the very middle of the deep blue stream, Brooke had attached a small golden cross, a gift from her father many years ago.

"Your cross . . . ," Candace said, touching the page. She didn't know what to make of it. Brooke treasured every gift her father had ever given her, yet she'd sacrificed possession of the lovely little cross, gluing it to the paper. A tear slipped down Candace's cheek, and all she could do was hold both of her children close.

"What's wrong? Don't you like it?" There was panic in her daughter's voice.

"I love it. I don't even have words to tell you how much."

She felt her doubt about God's goodness dissolving, her spirit cleansed. She'd been run aground at the same riverbank for four years now, and she imagined herself stepping into her life's river again to continue the journey. She didn't have to be overwhelmed by grief anymore. No matter what the future held, faith in God would sustain her.

"Thank You, Lord," she prayed out loud. "Help me to be worthy of the wonderful children You've given into my care."

"And please, God, say hello to Daddy for us and tell him how much we miss him," Brooke added.

"Amen!" Howie said, pumping his fist in the air. "Can I have a cookie now?"

Candace laughed, kissed Howie's forehead, and pulled both of her children close.

About the Authors

Pam Hanson and Barbara Andrews are a daughter/mother writing team. They have had nearly thirty books published together, including several for Guideposts in the series Tales from Grace Chapel Inn.

Pam's background is in journalism, and she previously taught at the university level for fifteen years. She and her college professor husband have two sons. Reading is her favorite pastime, and she enjoys being a volunteer youth leader at her church. Pam writes about faith and family at http://pamshanson.blogspot.com.

Previous to their partnership, Barbara had twenty-one novels published under her own name. She began her career by writing Sunday school stories and contributing to antiques publications. Currently, she writes a column and articles about collectible postcards. For the past twenty-five years, Barbara has conducted sales of antique postcards to benefit world hunger relief. She is the mother of four and the grandmother of eight. Barbara makes her home with Pam and her family in Nebraska.

Read on for a sneak peek of the next exciting and heartfelt book in *Stories from Hope Haven.*

It's available through Guideposts' direct mail program by calling Customer Service at (800) 932–2145.

THE *Heart* OF THE *Matter*

by

Leslie Gould

BY THE TIME ANABELLE SCOTT TURNED ONTO Jeffries Street and pulled behind Hope Haven Hospital—something she had been doing for the last thirty years—the rain was blowing sideways, pelting her car and swaying the budding trees toward the ground. Even though March had ended and April begun, the coming of spring still roared like a lion through northern Illinois.

She parked in the staff lot, pushed open the car door, and held her hood over her head as she forced the door shut with her foot. Before she could start her rush toward the entrance, a movement in the far corner of the parking lot caught her attention. There was Eddie Blaine wearing insulated coveralls and standing on a ladder, scrubbing the concrete wall. Was that graffiti?

She hurried toward him, dodging the puddles and streams of water crisscrossing the lot. "Eddie," she called. "It's too stormy for you to be out here!"

He held a wire brush midair and turned toward her, his broad shoulders squared. Black paint had been sprayed in broad strokes across the wall. "I think I'm going to have to power wash it."

"In this weather?"

Eddie lowered the brush in a gesture of defeat. "It sends a bad message to leave it. They say graffiti begets more graffiti. At least that's what the policeman who took the report said a little while ago."

Who'd ever target the hospital? This is terrible.

She was about to voice her thoughts when a gust of wind nearly knocked her off balance. "Eddie—" She was going to tell him he needed to get indoors, that it was crazy to be out in the middle of a storm, but she knew it wouldn't make any difference. The man was as dedicated to the care of the hospital as the nurses and doctors were dedicated to their patients. "Take care," she called out instead.

He pulled his stocking cap down over his ears, still holding the brush in his hand, and then waved good-bye as he smiled.

Anabelle increased her stride toward the hospital, buttoning the top of her coat with her free hand and then pulling her hood back in place, as James Bell steered his minivan into the lot. As usual, he looked upbeat but also tired. It might not have been so unusual for him at six thirty in the morning, but she still couldn't help wondering how he was doing under the stress of caring for Fern and all that was involved in raising two teenaged boys.

Anabelle remembered those child-rearing days well. Now she was excited to be entering a new stage of life: In five weeks or so, she would be a grandmother.

As she reached the sidewalk, James caught up with her, the hood of his jacket pulled over his graying hair, and said a quick hello as they reached the doors. He froze a moment, his gaze beyond her. "Is that Ainslee's car?"

Anabelle turned. A red Honda Civic was parked in the Emergency Room lot. She squinted through the rain. The antenna had a Mickey Mouse on the top, compliments of Ainslee's husband Doug. "Oh dear," Anabelle said, rushing through the door.

"She's probably fine," James said as he followed.

Anabelle pushed her hood from her head and turned toward the ER. Doug could be the one who was ill, not Ainslee. *Oh, Lord*, she silently prayed, *don't let it be either one*. But her heart told her it was her daughter—and the baby.

"Ainslee," she called out when she reached the ER. "Where are you?"

A plaid curtain halfway down the hall began to flutter and a moment later Doug peered around it. He had a baseball cap pulled tight on his head and wore an old sweatshirt and jeans. He looked exhausted.

"What's wrong?" Anabelle practically flew down the hall.

"We don't know yet." Doug began batting at the curtain, and as he did, Anabelle grabbed hold of it and yanked it to the side.

Ainslee sat in the middle of the bed. Her legs were crossed, and her dark red hair was twisted in a knot on top of her head.

"Hello, Mother." Her eyes were dull and tired. "I was having some pains, that's all." Ainslee wore a long-sleeved shirt of Doug's over her third-trimester bump.

James's deep voice came from behind her as he said hello and shook Doug's hand.

"What did the doctor say?" Anabelle stepped closer to the bed.

"We just got here," Doug answered.

There were so many possibilities—early labor, toxemia, a distressed fetus. "Where does it hurt, exactly?"

Ainslee touched her diaphragm with her free hand, resting it on top of her belly. "Up here. I couldn't sleep all night. I've never felt so miserable."

"Are you sure it's not heartburn?"

"I haven't eaten anything that would cause it."

"Sweetie, why didn't you call me?" Anabelle squeezed her daughter's hand.

Ainslee looked past her mother to Doug. "We didn't want to worry you if it turned out to be nothing."

"Worry me? What are you talking about? That's what mothers are for."

James cleared his throat. "I'm going to go," he said to Anabelle. "I'll stop by CCU and tell them you'll be late." He said his good-byes, and Anabelle thanked him for—she wasn't sure what. Maybe just for caring.

"You should call Dr. Carpenter. In fact—" Anabelle stepped toward the phone in the corner. "I can call her right now."

Ainslee scooted farther back on the bed, sitting up straighter. "I'm fine—feeling better already."

"You're not fine. You're in the ER."

Anabelle looked to Doug for help, but he glanced at Ainslee, then at the floor, then back at Anabelle and grimaced.

"All right," Anabelle said, dropping her hand to her side. Ainslee had always been the independent sort, not wanting to cause unnecessary fuss, so it was no surprise that she wanted to navigate this alone. But still it was hard for Anabelle to let her.

"I'll stop by and let you know what the doctor says," Ainslee said through a yawn, "before I leave."

Anabelle leaned forward, kissed her daughter on the forehead and then patted her belly, the cotton shirt soft on her hand, her daughter's abdomen taut. She felt a flutter of joy in her heart before being hit with the ever-present anxiety of worrying about her children—and soon-to-be grandchild.

She pulled her hand away. "Make sure and let me know—call upstairs if you need to. I can come down in a flash." She ducked between the curtains and hurried down the hall, glancing at her watch. She had eight minutes to get changed and be ready to take report. She increased her pace, pushing through the fire door toward the back stairs.

"Here I am," Anabelle said, a little out of breath as she slipped through the cardiac staff door. Debbie, the night charge nurse, sat at the head of the table.

"How's Ainslee?" Debbie's voice was soft. "James told us."

"I don't know," Anabelle said, lowering herself to a chair.

"Is it the baby?" Barbara asked.

Anabelle's throat constricted. "Maybe."

There was a moment of silence and then Debbie continued with report. Anabelle willed herself to concentrate on the words of her colleagues and to stop obsessing about Ainslee and the baby.

At 11:45 AM, Anabelle tried to call her husband again. She'd already left two messages but didn't bother to leave a third. Cameron was likely in the barn puttering around. After hanging up the phone, she tried to fathom why it would take Ainslee more than five hours in the ER as she turned her attention to the staff schedule.

Anabelle stared at the computer screen for a long time. She had never been tempted before to check the records of a patient who was not hers; it was strictly against policy, even though it was her daughter. The offense could cost Anabelle her job if she gave in. To distract herself, she stood and decided to grab a cup of coffee, telling Barbara, the unit secretary, that she would be right back. A quick trip to the staff lounge would loosen her up a little.

As she logged off the computer, Barbara whispered, "Look who's here."

Anabelle's head shot up. Ainslee was walking toward her, her down jacket in her hands in front of her belly. Anabelle tried to read her daughter's face.

"What's going on? What did the doctor say?" Anabelle asked.

Ainslee glanced at Barbara and then whispered, "I'll tell you later."

"I want to hear everything right now. Do you have time for an early lunch?"

Ainslee tilted her head and a strand of hair came loose from her haphazard bun and brushed against her face. She tucked it behind her ear. "I am hungry."

"There's a good pasta bar here on Mondays."

Ainslee turned toward the clock on the wall and then back. "Boy, I was down there a long time. No wonder I'm starving."

"Here, let me carry your coat," said Anabelle, gathering the bulky coat into her arms.

Anabelle and Ainslee headed to the cafeteria, where Anabelle filled her plate with salad while Ainslee cruised the pasta bar. Anabelle smiled at the sight of her daughter's tray, which was heaped with pasta, a salad, bread sticks, custard, and a carton of milk. Anabelle knew that there was once a time that she could eat like that too. As she tucked her wallet back into her purse, Anabelle spotted a cup of coffee on Ainslee's tray.

"I bet you can't wait to get back to drinking regular coffee."

Ainslee lifted her tray. "This is regular."

"Sweetie." Anabelle accidentally jostled her purse against her tray and then steadied it. "The caffeine isn't good for the baby."

"No, I think it's fine."

"Honey, I know it's not." Anabelle led the way to the far booth where she'd deposited the coat before Ainslee could answer. When Anabelle was pregnant, she hadn't been allowed a drop of regular coffee—only decaf. She settled onto the bench seat, hoping the privacy would encourage a heart-to-heart conversation. Ainslee arrived a moment later.

"I think things have changed since you were pregnant," Ainslee said, sliding onto the opposite bench. "You know," she said with a teasing tone, "it has been a long time."

Anabelle chuckled. It didn't seem like it had been that long to her. And she'd said her piece, so she'd drop it for now; but she was positive Ainslee shouldn't have caffeine.

"Thanks for the food." Ainslee shoved her jacket toward the wall. "I don't think I could have made it home, I'm so hungry."

Candace waved from across the room and headed toward them. "There you are," she said, her highlighted hair bobbing against her neck. "How are you doing?"

"Good. Starving."

Candace laughed. "Eat. Don't let me stop you."

Ainslee plunged her fork into the pasta.

"But go easy on the red sauce. That might make the indigestion come back."

"Indigestion?" Anabelle sputtered.

Ainslee's face turned red.

Candace smiled and tucked a strand of hair behind her ear. "You know I had a couple of bad bouts when I was pregnant with Brooke too. It's amazing how the most common thing can be a really big deal when you're pregnant." Candace seemed oblivious to Ainslee's embarrassment and to Anabelle's shock. "Okay, well, it was good to see you, regardless of the circumstances. I just hope I'm working when you deliver."

Ainslee said she hoped the same and then Candace said a quick good-bye.

"Indigestion?" Anabelle asked again.

Ainslee's voice was nearly a whisper. "Mother."

"Why didn't you call me?" Anabelle felt embarrassed that her daughter would go to the ER because of indigestion, but then it suddenly seemed hilarious and she stifled a laugh.

"Mother." Ainslee shook her head.

"You should have called me, honey. Even if it was the middle of the night." Anabelle was overcome with relief. It was only indigestion. Ainslee and the baby really were fine. "I'm always available."

"Please stop," Ainslee said, her fork midair. "You know why I didn't call?"

Anabelle shook her head. *I probably don't want to know*, she thought.

"Because I feel like you're always criticizing me."

"What do you mean?"

"It's implied in all the advice you're always dishing out."

"I'm just trying to share what I've already learned, as a nurse and a mom." She paused. "Ains, I'm just trying to help."

Ainslee slid back from the table and leaned against the back of the bench, exhaling loudly.

"Eat." Anabelle pointed her fork at her daughter's plate. "You and the baby both need it."

"I'm not hungry anymore." Ainslee slipped into her coat and grabbed her purse. "I need to go get cleaned up and go into work."

"You need a nap, sweetie. That's what you need."

Ainslee stood. "You're doing it again."

Anabelle cringed.

"Mother, I'm thirty years old."

Anabelle pushed her tray to the middle of the table and stood too. "I don't mean to, honestly." Someday Ainslee would understand, someday when her baby was grown. "I'll call you when I get off work, to see how you are." Anabelle reached out to hug her daughter, and Ainslee relaxed for just a moment but then pulled back and picked up her tray with the barely touched food and the untouched coffee, resting it on her belly.

Anabelle sat back down and watched her daughter walk toward the rack of dirty trays. Ainslee slid hers into the slot and then turned and waved. She looked exhausted.

Anabelle took another bite of salad, upset by Ainslee's proclamation. She'd behaved beautifully all morning. She'd stayed out of the ER, and for goodness' sake, it *had* turned out to be heartburn. She'd been right all along. She could have diagnosed it over the phone at 2:00 AM and saved Ainslee a morning at the hospital.

But she couldn't control her kids, not Ainslee or Kirstie or Evan. She'd known that for years. But becoming a grandparent was new territory for her. She felt so protective of this new baby. She smiled in spite of herself. She was going to be a grandmother! Ainslee would surely come around to her sound advice. All her daughter needed right now was a nap.

A Note from the Editors

Guideposts, a nonprofit organization, touches millions of lives every day through products and services that inspire, encourage and uplift. Our magazines, books, prayer network and outreach programs help people connect their faith-filled values to their daily lives.

Your purchase of *Stories from Hope Haven* does make a difference! To comfort hospitalized children, Guideposts Outreach has created Comfort Kits for free distribution. A hospital can be a very scary place for sick children. With all the hustle and bustle going on around them, the strange surroundings, and the pain they're experiencing, is it any wonder kids need a little relief?

Inside each easy-to-carry Comfort Kit is a prayer card, a journal, a pack of crayons, an "I'm Special" wristband to wear alongside the hospital-issued one and a plush golden star pillow to cuddle. It's a welcome gift and has a powerful effect in helping to soothe a child's fears.

To learn more about our many nonprofit outreach programs, please visit www.guidepostsfoundation.org.